Bruce

by Albert Payson Terhune

Originally published in 1920.

TO MY TEN BEST FRIENDS:

Who are far wiser in their way and far better in
every way, than I; and yet who have not the wisdom
to know it Who do not merely think I am perfect,
but who are calmly and permanently convinced of
my perfection;--and this in spite of fifty disillusions
a day Who are frantically happy at my coming and
bitterly woebegone in my absence Who never bore
me and never are bored by me Who never talk about
themselves and who always listen with rapturous
interest to anything I may say Who, having no
conventional standards, have no respectability; and
who, having no conventional consciences, have no
sins Who teach me finer lessons in loyalty, in
patience, in true courtesy, in unselfishness, in divine
forgiveness, in pluck and in abiding good spirits
than do all the books I have ever read and all the
other models I have studied Who have not deigned
to waste time and eyesight in reading a word of
mine and who will not bother to read this verbose
tribute to themselves In short, to the most gloriously
satisfactory chums who ever appealed to human
vanity and to human desire for companionship

TO OUR TEN SUNNYBANK COLLIES MY
STORY IS GRATEFULLY AND
AFFECTIONATELY DEDICATED

CHAPTER I.

The Coming Of Bruce

She was beautiful. And she had a heart and a soul--
which were a curse. For without such a heart and
soul, she might have found the tough life-battle less
bitterly hard to fight.

But the world does queer things--damnable things--
to hearts that are so tenderly all-loving and to souls
that are so trustfully and forgivingly friendly as
hers.

Her "pedigree name" was Rothsay Lass. She was a
collie--daintily fragile of build, sensitive of nostril,
furrily tawny of coat. Her ancestry was as flawless
as any in Burke's Peerage.

If God had sent her into the world with a pair of
tulip ears and with a shade less width of brain-space
she might have been cherished and coddled as a
potential bench-show winner, and in time might
even have won immortality by the title of
"CHAMPION Rothsay Lass."

But her ears pricked rebelliously upward, like those
of her earliest ancestors, the wolves. Nor could
manipulation lure their stiff cartilages into drooping
as bench show fashion demands. The average show-
collie's ears have a tendency to prick. By weights
and plasters, and often by torture, this tendency is
overcome. But never when the cartilage is as
unyielding as was Lass's.

Her graceful head harked back in shape to the days
when collies had to do much independent thinking,
as sheep-guards, and when they needed more
brainroom than is afforded by the borzoi skull
sought after by modern benchshow experts.

Wherefore, Lass had no hope whatever of winning
laurels in the show-ring or of attracting a high price
from some rich fancier. She was tabulated, from
babyhood, as a "second"--in other words, as a faulty
specimen in a litter that should have been faultless.

These "seconds" are as good to look at, from a
layman's view, as is any international champion.
And their offspring are sometimes as perfect as are
those of the finest specimens. But, lacking the
arbitrary "points" demanded by show-judges, the
"seconds" are condemned to obscurity, and to sell
as pets.

If Lass had been a male dog, her beauty and sense
and lovableness would have found a ready
purchaser for her. For nine pet collies out of ten are
"seconds"; and splendid pets they make for the most
part.

But Lass, at the very start, had committed the
unforgivable sin of being born a female. Therefore,
no pet-seeker wanted to buy her. Even when she
was offered for sale at half the sum asked for her
less handsome brothers, no one wanted her.

A mare--or the female of nearly any species except
the canine-- brings as high and as ready a price as
does the male. But never the female dog. Except for

breeding, she is not wanted.

This prejudice had its start in Crusader days, some thousand years ago. Up to that time, all through the civilized world, a female dog had been more popular as a pet than a male. The Mohammedans (to whom, by creed, all dogs are unclean) gave their European foes the first hint that a female dog was the lowest thing on earth.

The Saracens despised her, as the potential mother of future dogs. And they loathed her accordingly. Back to Europe came the Crusaders, bearing only three lasting memorials of their contact with the Moslems. One of the three was a sneering contempt for all female dogs.

There is no other pet as loving, as quick of wit, as loyal, as staunchly brave and as companionable as the female collie. She has all the male's best traits and none of his worst. She has more in common, too, with the highest type of woman than has any other animal alive. (This, with all due respect to womanhood.)

Prejudice has robbed countless dog-lovers of the joy of owning such a pal. In England the female pet dog has at last begun to come into her own. Here she has not. The loss is ours.

And so back to Lass.

When would-be purchasers were conducted to the puppy-run at the Rothsay kennels, Lass and her six brethren and sisters were wont to come galloping to the gate to welcome the strangers. For the pups were only three months old--an age when every event is thrillingly interesting, and everybody is a friend. Three times out of five, the buyer's eye would single Lass from the rollicking and fluffy mass of puppyhood.

She was so pretty, so wistfully appealing, so free from fear (and from bumptiousness as well) and carried herself so daintily, that one's heart warmed to her. The visitor would point her out. The kennel-man would reply, flatteringly--

"Yes, she sure is one fine pup!"

The purchaser never waited to hear the end of the sentence, before turning to some other puppy. The pronoun, "she," had killed forever his dawning fancy for the little beauty.

The four males of the litter were soon sold; for there is a brisk and a steady market for good collie pups. One of the two other females died. Lass's remaining sister began to "shape up" with show-possibilities, and was bought by the owner of another kennel. Thus, by the time she was five months old, Lass was left alone in the puppy-run.

She mourned her playmates. It was cold, at night, with no other cuddly little fur-ball to snuggle down to. It was stupid, with no one to help her work off her five-months spirits in a romp. And Lass missed the dozens of visitors that of old had come to the run.

The kennel-men felt not the slightest interest in her. Lass meant nothing to them, except the work of feeding her and of keeping an extra run in order. She was a liability, a nuisance.

Lass used to watch with pitiful eagerness for the attendants' duty-visits to the run. She would gallop joyously up to them, begging for a word or a caress, trying to tempt them into a romp, bringing them peaceofferings in the shape of treasured bones she had buried for her own future use. But all this gained her nothing.

A careless word at best--a grunt or a shove at worst were her only rewards. For the most part, the men with the feed-trough or the water-pail ignored her bounding and wrigglingly eager welcome as completely as though she were a part of the kennel furnishings. Her short daily "exercise scamper" in the open was her nearest approach to a good time.

Then came a day when again a visitor stopped in front of Lass's run. He was not much of a visitor, being a pallid and rather shabbily dressed lad of twelve, with a brand-new chain and collar in his hand.

"You see," he was confiding to the bored kennel-man who had been detailed by the foreman to take him around the kennels, "when I got the check from Uncle Dick this morning, I made up my mind, first thing, to buy a dog with it, even if it took every cent. But then I got to thinking I'd need something to fasten him with, so he wouldn't run away before he learned to like me and want to stay with me. So when I got the check cashed at the store, I got this collar and chain."

"Are you a friend of the boss?" asked the kennel-man.

"The boss?" echoed the boy. "You mean the man who owns this place? No, sir. But when I've walked past, on the road, I've seen his 'Collies for Sale' sign, lots of times. Once I saw some of them being exercised. They were the wonderfulest dogs I ever saw. So the minute I got the money for the check, I came here. I told the man in the front yard I wanted to buy a dog. He's the one who turned me over to you. I wish--OH!" he broke off in rapture, coming to a halt in front of Lass's run. "Look! Isn't he a dandy?"

Lass had trotted hospitably forward to greet the guest. Now she was standing on her hind legs, her front paws alternately supporting her fragile weight on the wire of the fence and waving welcomingly toward the boy. Unknowingly, she was bidding for a master. And her wistful friendliness struck a note of response in the little fellow's heart. For he, too, was lonesome, much of the time, as is the fate of a sickly only child in an overbusy home. And he had the true craving of the lonely for dog comradeship.

He thrust his none-too-clean hand through the wire mesh and patted the puppy's silky head. Lass wiggled ecstatically under the unfamiliar caress. All at once, in the boy's eyes, she became quite the most wonderful animal and the very most desirable pet on earth,

"He's great!" sighed the youngster in admiration; adding naïvely: "Is he Champion Rothsay Chief-- the one whose picture was in The Bulletin last Sunday?"

The kennel-man laughed noisily. Then he checked his mirth, for professional reasons, as he remembered the nature of the boy's quest and foresaw a bare possibility of getting rid of the unwelcome Lass.

"Nope," he said. "This isn't Chief. If it was, I guess your Uncle Dick's check would have to have four figures in it before you could make a deal. But this is one of Chief's daughters. This is Rothsay Lass. A grand little girl, ain't she? Say,"--in a confidential whisper,--"since you've took a fancy for her, maybe I could coax the old man into lettin' you have her at an easy price. He was plannin' to sell her for a hundred or so. But he goes pretty much by what I say. He might let her go for--How much of a check did you say your uncle sent you?"

"Twelve dollars," answered the boy,--"one for each year. Because I'm named for him. It's my birthday, you know. But--but a dollar of it went for the chain and the collar. How much do you suppose the gentleman would want for Rothsay Lass?"

The kennel-man considered for a moment. Then he went back to the house, leaving the lad alone at the gate of the run. Eleven dollars, for a high-pedigreed collie pup, was a joke price. But no one else wanted Lass, and her feed was costing more every day. According to Rothsay standards, the list of brood-females was already complete. Even as a gift, the kennels would be making money by getting rid of the prick-eared "second." Wherefore he went to consult with the foreman.

Left alone with Lass, the boy opened the gate and went into the run. A little to his surprise Lass neither shrank from him nor attacked him. She danced about his legs in delight, varying this by jumping up and trying to lick his excited face. Then she thrust her cold nose into the cup of his hand as a plea to be petted.

When the kennel-man came back, the boy was sitting on the dusty ground of the run, and Lass was curled up rapturously in his lap, learning how to shake hands at his order.

"You can have her, the boss says," vouchsafed the kennel-man. "Where's the eleven dollars?"

By this graceless speech Dick Hazen received the key to the Seventh Paradise, and a life-membership in the world-wide Order of Dog-Lovers.

The homeward walk, for Lass and her new master, was no walk at all, but a form of spiritual levitation. The half-mile pilgrimage consumed a full hour of time. Not that Lass hung back or rebelled at her first taste of collar and chain! These petty annoyances went unfelt in the wild joy of a real walk, and in the infinitely deeper happiness of knowing her friendship-famine was appeased at last.

The walk was long for various reasons--partly

because, in her frisking gyrations, Lass was forever tangling the new chain around Dick's thin ankles; partly because he stopped, every block or so, to pat her or to give her further lessons in the art of shaking hands. Also there were admiring boy-acquaintances along the way, to whom the wonderful pet must be exhibited.

At last Dick turned in at the gate of a cheap bungalow on a cheap street--a bungalow with a discouraged geranium plot in its pocket-handkerchief front yard, and with a double line of drying clothes in the no larger space behind the house.

As Dick and his chum rounded the house, a woman emerged from between the two lines of flapping sheets, whose hanging she had been superintending. She stopped at sight of her son and the dog.

"Oh!" she commented with no enthusiasm at all. "Well, you did it, hey? I was hoping you'd have better sense, and spend your check on a nice new suit or something. He's kind of pretty, though," she went on, the puppy's friendliness and beauty wringing the word of grudging praise from her. "What kind of a dog is he? And you're sure he isn't savage, aren't you?"

"Collie," answered Dick proudly. "Pedigreed collie! You bet she isn't savage, either. Why, she's an angel. She minds me already. See--shake hands, Lass!" "Lass!" ejaculated Mrs. Hazen. "'SHE!' Dick, you don't mean to tell me you've gone and bought yourself a--a FEMALE dog?"

The woman spoke in the tone of horrified contempt
that might well have been hers had she found a
rattlesnake and a brace of toads in her son's pocket.
And she lowered her voice, as is the manner of her
kind when forced to speak of the unspeakable. She
moved back from the puppy's politely out-thrust
forepaw as from the passing of a garbage cart.

"A female dog!" she reiterated. "Well, of all the
chuckle-heads! A nasty FEMALE dog, with your
birthday money!"

"She's not one bit nasty!" flamed Dick, burying the
grubby fingers of his right hand protectively in the
fluffy mass of the puppy's half-grown ruff. "She's
the dandiest dog ever! She--"

"Don't talk back to me!" snapped Mrs. Hazen.
"Here! Turn right around and take her to the cheats
who sold her to you. Tell them to keep her and give
you the good money you paid for her. Take her out
of my yard this minute! Quick!"

A hot mist of tears sprang into the boy's eyes. Lass,
with the queer intuition that tells a female collie
when her master is unhappy, whined softly and
licked his clenched hand.

"I--aw, PLEASE, Ma!" he begged chokingly.
"PLEASE! It's--it's my birthday, and everything.
Please let me keep her. I--I love her better than
'most anything there is. Can't I please keep her?
Please!"

"You heard what I said," returned his mother curtly.

The washerwoman, who one day a week lightened
Mrs. Hazen's household labors, waddled into view
from behind the billows of wind-swirled clothes.
She was an excellent person, and was built for
endurance rather than for speed. At sight of Lass
she paused in real interest.

"My!" she exclaimed with flattering approval. "So
you got your dog, did you? You didn't waste no
time. And he's sure a handsome little critter.
Whatcher goin' to call him?"

"It's not a him, Irene," contradicted Mrs. Hazen,
with another modest lowering of her strong voice.
"It's a HER. And I'm sending Dick back with her, to
where she came from. I've got my opinion of people
who will take advantage of a child's ignorance, by
palming off a horrid female dog on him, too. Take
her away, Dick. I won't have her here another
minute. You hear me?"

"Please, Ma!" stammered Dick, battling with his
desire to cry. "Aw, PLEASE! I--I--"

"Your ma's right, Dick," chimed in the
washerwoman, her first interested glance at the
puppy changing to one of refined and lofty scorn.
"Take her back. You don't want any female dogs
around. No nice folks do."

"Why not?" demanded the boy in sudden hopeless
anger as he pressed lovingly the nose Lass thrust so
comfortingly into his hand. "WHY don't we want a
female dog around? Folks have female cats around
them, and female women. Why isn't a female dog--"

"That will do, Dick!" broke in his shocked mother. "Take her away."

"I won't," said the boy, speaking very slowly, and with no excitement at all.

A slap on the side of his head, from his mother's punitive palm, made him stagger a little. Her hand was upraised for a second installment of rebellion-quelling--when a slender little body flashed through the air and landed heavily against her chest. A set of white puppy-teeth all but grazed her wrathful red face.

Lass, who never before had known the impulse to attack, had jumped to the rescue of the beaten youngster whom she had adopted as her god. The woman screeched in terror. Dick flung an arm about the furry whirlwind that was seeking to avenge his punishment, and pulled the dog back to his side.

Mrs. Hazen's shriek, and the obbligato accompaniment of the washerwoman, made an approaching man quicken his steps as he strolled around the side of the house. The newcomer was Dick's father, superintendent of the local bottling works. On his way home to lunch, he walked in on a scene of hysteria.

"Kill her, sir!" bawled the washerwoman, at sight of him. "Kill her! She's a mad dog. She just tried to kill Miz' Hazen!"

"She didn't do anything of the kind!" wailed Dick. "She was pertecting me. Ma hit me; and Lass--"

"Ed!" tearily proclaimed Mrs. Hazen, "if you don't send for a policeman to shoot that filthy beast, I'll--"

"Hold on!" interrupted the man, at a loss to catch the drift of these appeals, by reason of their all being spoken in a succession so rapid as to make a single blurred sentence. "Hold on! What's wrong? And where did the pup come from? He's a looker, all right a cute little cuss. What's the row?"

With the plangently useless iterations of a Greek chorus, the tale was flung at him, piecemeal and in chunks, and in a triple key. When presently he understood, Hazen looked down for a moment at the puppy--which was making sundry advances of a shy but friendly nature toward him. Then he looked at the boy, and noted Dick's hero-effort to choke back the onrush of babyish sobs. And then, with a roughly tolerant gesture, he silenced the two raucous women, who were beginning the tale over again for the third time.

"I see," he said. "I see. I see how it is. Needn't din it at me any more, folks. And I see Dicky's side of it, too. Yes, and I see the pup's side of it. I know a lot about dogs. That pup isn't vicious. She knows she belongs to Dick. You lammed into him, and she took up and defended him. That's all there is to the 'mad- dog' part of it."

"But Ed--" sputtered his wife.

"Now, you let ME do the talking, Sade!" he insisted, half- grinning, yet more than half grimly. "I'm the boss here. If I'm not, then it's safe to listen

to me till the boss gets here. And we're goin' to do
whatever I say we are--without any back-talk or
sulks, either. It's this way: Your brother gave the
boy a birthday check. We promised he could spend
it any way he had a mind to. He said he wanted a
dog, didn't he? And I said, 'Go to it!' didn't I ? Well,
he got the dog. Just because it happens to be a she,
that's no reason why he oughtn't to be allowed to
keep it. And he can. That goes."

"Oh, Dad!" squealed Dick in grateful heroworship.
"You're a brick! I'm not ever going to forget this, so
long as I live. Say, watch her shake hands, Dad! I've
taught her, already, to--"

"Ed Hazen!" loudly protested his wife. "Of all the
softies! You haven't backbone enough for a prune.
And if my orders to my own son are going to be--"

"That'll be all, Sade!" interposed the man stiffly--
adding: "By the way, I got a queer piece of news to
tell you. Come into the kitchen a minute."

Grumbling, rebellious, scowling,--yet unable to
resist the lure of a "queer piece of news," Mrs.
Hazen followed her husband indoors, leaving Dick
and his pet to gambol deliriously around the
clothes-festooned yard in celebration of their
victory.

"Listen here, old girl!" began Hazen the moment the
kitchen door was shut behind them. "Use some
sense, can't you? I gave you the wink, and you
wouldn't catch on. So I had to make the grandstand
play. I'm no more stuck on having a measly she-dog

around here than you are. And we're not going to
have her, either. But--"

"Then why did you say you were going to? Why did
you make a fool of me before Irene and
everything?" she demanded, wrathful yet
bewildered.

"It's the boy's birthday, isn't it?" urged Hazen. "And
I'd promised him, hadn't I? And, last time he had
one of those 'turns,' didn't Doc Colfax say we
mustn't let him fret and worry any more'n we could
help? Well, if he had to take that dog back to-day,
it'd have broke his heart. He'd have felt like we
were his enemies, and he'd never have felt the same
to us again. And it might have hurt his health too--
the shock and all. So--"

"But I tell you," she persisted, "I won't have a dirty
little female--"

"We aren't going to," he assured her. "Keep your
hair on, till I've finished. Tonight, after Dick's
asleep, I'm going to get rid of her. He'll wake up in
the morning and find she's gone; and the door'll be
open. He'll think she's run away. He'll go looking
for her, and he'll keep on hoping to find her. So
that'll ease the shock, you see, by letting him down
bit by bit, instead of snatching his pet away from
him violent-like. And he won't hold it up against
US, either, as he would the other way. I can offer a
reward for her, too."

There was a long and thought-crammed pause. The
woman plunged deep into the silences as her fat

brain wrought over the suggestion. Then--

"Maybe you HAVE got just a few grains of sense, after all, Ed," grudgingly vouchsafed Mrs. Hazen. "It isn't a bad idea. Only he'll grieve a lot for her."

"He'll be hoping, though," said her husband. "He'll be hoping all the while. That always takes the razor-edge off of grieving. Leave it to me."

That was the happiest day Dick Hazen had ever known. And it was the first actively happy day in all Lass's five months of life.

Boy and dog spent hours in a ramble through the woods. They began Lass's education--which was planned to include more intricate tricks than a performing elephant and a troupe of circus dogs could hope to learn in a lifetime. They became sworn chums. Dick talked to Lass as if she were human. She amazed the enraptured boy by her cleverness and spirits. His initiation to the dog-masters' guild was joyous and complete.

It was a tired and ravenous pair of friends who scampered home at dinner-time that evening. The pallor was gone from Dick's face. His cheeks were glowing, and his eyes shone. He ate greedily. His parents looked covertly at each other. And the self-complacency lines around Hazen's mouth blurred.

Boy and dog went to bed early, being blissfully sleepy and full of food--also because another and longer woodland ramble was scheduled for the morrow.

Timidly Dick asked leave to have Lass sleep on the foot of his cot-bed. After a second telegraphing of glances, his parents consented. Half an hour later the playmates were sound asleep, the puppy snuggling deep in the hollow of her master's arm, her furry head across his thin chest.

It was in this pose that Hazen found them when, late in the evening, he tiptoed into Dick's cubby-hole room. He gazed down at the slumberous pair for a space, while he fought and conquered an impulse toward fair play. Then he stooped to pick up the dog.

Lass, waking at the slight creak of a floorboard, lifted her head. At sight of the figure leaning above her adored master, the lip curled back from her white teeth. Far down in her throat a growl was born. Then she recognized the intruder as the man who had petted her and fed her that evening. The growl died in her throat, giving place to a welcoming thump or two of her bushy tail. Dick stirred uneasily.

Patting the puppy lightly on her upraised head, Hazen picked up Lass in his arms and tiptoed out of the room with her. Mistaking this move for a form of caress, she tried to lick his face. The man winced.

Downstairs and out into the street Hazen bore his trustful little burden, halting only to put on his hat, and for a whispered word with his wife. For nearly a mile he carried the dog. Lass greatly enjoyed the ride. She was pleasantly tired, and it was nice to be carried thus, by some one who was so considerate as to save her the bother of walking.

At the edge of the town, Hazen set her on the ground and at once began to walk rapidly away in the direction of home. He had gone perhaps fifty yards when Lass was gamboling merrily around his feet. A kick sent the dismayed and agonized puppy flying through the air like a whimpering catapult, and landed her against a bank with every atom of breath knocked out of her. Before she had fairly struck ground,--before she could look about her,-- Hazen had doubled around a corner and had vanished.

At a run, he made for home, glad the unpleasant job was over. At the door his wife met him.

"Well," she demanded, "did you drown her in the canal, the way you said?"

"No," he confessed sheepishly, "I didn't exactly drown her. You see, she nestled down into my arms so cozy and trusting-like, that I--well, I fixed it so she'll never show up around here again. Trust me to do a job thoroughly, if I do it at all. I--"

A dramatic gesture from Mrs. Hazen's stubby forefinger interrupted him. He followed the finger's angry point. Close at his side stood Lass, wagging her tail and staring expectantly up at him.

With her keen power of scent, it had been no exploit at all to track the man over a mile of unfamiliar ground. Already she had forgiven the kick or had put it down to accident on his part. And

at the end of her eager chase, she was eager for a
word of greeting.

"I'll be--" gurgled Hazen, blinking stupidly.

"I guess you will be," conceded his wife. "If that's
the 'thorough' way you do your jobs at the factory--"

"Say," he mumbled in a sort of wondering appeal,
"is there any HUMAN that would like to trust a
feller so much as to risk another ribcracking kick,
just for the sake of being where he is? I almost
wish--"

But the wish was unspoken. Hazen was a true
American husband. He feared his wife more than he
loved fairness. And his wife's glare was full upon
him. With a grunt he picked Lass up by the neck,
tucked her under his arm and made off through the
dark.

He did not take the road toward the canal, however.
Instead he made for the railroad tracks. He
remembered how, as a lad, he had once gotten rid of
a mangy cat, and he resolved to repeat the exploit. It
was far more merciful to the puppy--or at least, to
Hazen's conscience,--than to pitch Lass into the
slimy canal with a stone tied to her neck.

A line of freight cars--"empties"--was on a siding, a
short distance above the station. Hazen walked
along the track, trying the door of each car he
passed. The fourth he came to was unlocked. He
slid back the newly greased side door, thrust Lass
into the chilly and black interior and quickly slid

shut the door behind her. Then with the silly feeling of having committed a crime, he stumbled away through the darkness at top speed.

A freight car has a myriad uses, beyond the carrying of legitimate freight. From time immemorial, it has been a favorite repository for all manner of illicit flotsam and jetsam human or otherwise.

Its popularity with tramps and similar derelicts has long been a theme for comic paper and vaudeville jest. Though, heaven knows, the inside of a moving box-car has few jocose features, except in the imagination of humorous artist or vaudevillian!

But a far more frequent use for such cars has escaped the notice of the public at large. As any old railroader can testify, trainhands are forever finding in box-cars every genus and species of stray.

These finds range all the way from cats and dogs and discarded white rabbits and canaries, to goats. Dozens of babies have been discovered, wailing and deserted, in box-car recesses; perhaps a hundred miles from the siding where, furtively, the tiny human bundle was thrust inside some conveniently unlatched side door.

A freight train offers glittering chances for the disposal of the Unwanted. More than once a slain man or woman has been sent along the line, in this grisly but effective fashion, far beyond the reach of recognition.

Hazen had done nothing original or new in

depositing the luckless collie pup in one of these
wheeled receptacles. He was but following an old--
established custom, familiar to many in his line of
life. There was no novelty to it,--except to Lass.

The car was dark and cold and smelly. Lass hated it.
She ran to its door. Here she found a gleam of hope
for escape and for return to the home where every
one that day had been so kind to her. Hazen had
shut the door with such vehemence that it had
rebounded. The hasp was down, and so the catch
had not done its duty. The door had slid open a few
inches from the impetus of Hazen's shove.

It was not wide enough open to let Lass jump out,
but it was wide enough for her to push her nose
through. And by vigorous thrusting, with her
triangular head as a wedge, she was able to widen
the aperture, inch by inch. In less than three minutes
she had broadened it far enough for her to wriggle
out of the car and leap to the side of the track. There
she stood bewildered.

A spring snow was drifting down from the sulky
sky. The air was damp and penetrating. By reason
of the new snow the scent of Hazen's departing
footsteps was blotted out. Hazen himself was no
longer in sight. As Lass had made the journey from
house to tracks with her head tucked confidingly
under her kidnaper's arm, she had not noted the
direction. She was lost.

A little way down the track the station lights were
shining with misty warmth through the snow.
Toward these lights the puppy trotted.

Under the station eaves, and waiting to be taken
aboard the almost-due eleven-forty express, several
crates and parcels were grouped. One crate was the
scene of much the same sort of escape- -drama that
Lass had just enacted.

The crate was big and comfortable, bedded down
with soft sacking and with "insets" at either side
containing food and water. But commodious as was
the box, the unwonted confinement did not at all
please its occupant--a temperamental and highly
bred young collie in process of shipment from the
Rothsay Kennels to a purchaser forty miles up the
line.

This collie, wearying of the delay and the loneliness
and the strange quarters, had begun to plunge from
one side of the crate to the other in an effort to
break out. A carelessly nailed slat gave away under
the impact. The dog scrambled through the gap and
proceeded to gallop homeward through the snow.

Ten seconds later, Lass, drawn by the lights and by
the scent of the other dog, came to the crate. She
looked in. There, made to order for her, was a nice
bed. There, too, were food and drink to appease the
ever-present appetite of a puppy. Lass writhed her
way in through the gap as easily as the former
occupant had crawled out.

After doing due justice to the broken puppy biscuits
in the inset-trough, she curled herself up for a nap.

The clangor and glare of the oncoming express
awakened her. She cowered in one corner of the

crate. Just then two station-hands began to move the express packages out to the edge of the platform. One of them noticed the displaced board of the crate. He drove home its loosened nails with two sharp taps from a monkey-wrench, glanced inside to make certain the dog had not gotten out, and presently hoisted the crate aboard the express- car.

Two hours later the crate was unloaded at a waystation. At seven in the morning an expressman drove two miles with it to a country-home, a mile or so from the village where Lass had been disembarked from the train.

An eager knot of people--the Mistress, the Master and two gardeners--crowded expectantly around the crate as it was set down on the lawn in front of The Place's veranda. The latch was unfastened, and the crate's top was lifted back on its hinges.

Out stepped Lass,--tired, confused, a little frightened, but eagerly willing to make friends with a world which she still insisted on believing was friendly. It is hard to shake a collie pup's inborn faith in the friendliness of mankind, but once shaken, it is more than shaken. It is shattered beyond hope of complete mending.

For an instant she stood thus, looking in timid appeal from one to another of the faces about her. These faces were blank enough as they returned her gaze. The glad expectancy was wiped from them as with a sponge. It was the Master who first found voice.

"And THAT'S Rothsay Princess!" he snorted indignantly. "That's the pup worth two hundred dollars at eight months, 'because she has every single good point of Champion Rothsay Chief and not a flaw from nostril to tail-tip'! Rothsay wrote those very words about her, you remember. And he's supposed to be the most dependable man in the collie business! Lord! She's undersized--no bigger than a five monther ! And she's prick-eared and apple- domed; and her head's as wide as a church door!"

Apparently these humans were not glad to see her. Lass was grieved at their cold appraisal and a little frightened by the Master's tone of disgust. Yet she was eager, as ever, to make a good impression and to lure people into liking her. Shyly she walked up to the Mistress and laid one white little paw on her knee.

Handshaking was Lass's one accomplishment. It had been taught her by Dick. It had pleased the boy. He had been proud of her ability to do it. Perhaps it might also please these strangers. And after the odd fashion of all new arrivals who came to The Place, Lass picked out the Mistress, rather than any one else, as a potential friend.

The Mistress had ever roused the impatience of collie experts by looking past the showier "points" of a dog and into the soul and brain and disposition that lay behind them. So now she looked; and what she saw in Lass's darkly wistful eyes established the intruder's status at The Place.

"Let her stay!" pleaded the Mistress as the Master growled something about bundling the dog into her crate again and sending her back to the Rothsay Kennels. "Let her stay, please! She's a dear."

"But we're not breeding 'dears,'" observed the Master. "We planned to breed a strain of perfect collies. And this is a mutt!"

"Her pedigree says there's no better collie blood in America," denied the Mistress. "And even if she happens to be a 'second,' that's no sign her puppies will be seconds. See how pretty and loving and wise she is. DO keep her!"

Which of course settled the matter.

Up the lawn, from his morning swim in the lake, strolled a great mahogany-and-white collie. At sight of Lass he lowered his head for a charge. He was king of The Place's dogs, this mighty thoroughbred, Sunnybank Lad. And he did not welcome canine intruders.

But he halted midway in his dash toward the puppy who frisked forth so gayly to meet him. For he recognized her as a female. And man is the only animal that will molest the female of his species.

The fiercely silent charge was changed in a trice to a coldly civil touching of noses, and the majestic wagging of a plumy tail. After which, side by side, the two collies--big and little- -old and new--walked up to the veranda, to be petted by the humans who had so amusedly watched their encounter.

"See!" exclaimed the Mistress, in triumph. "Lad has accepted her. He vouches for her. That ought to be enough for any one!"

Thus it was that Lass found a home.

As she never yet had been taught to know her name, she learned readily to respond to the title of "Princess." And for several months life went on evenly and happily for her.

Indeed, life was always wondrous pleasant, there at The Place,-- for humans and for animals alike. A fire-blue lake bordered the grounds on two sides. Behind stretched the forest. And on every side arose the soft green mountains, hemming in and brooding over The Place as though they loved it. In the winter evenings there was the huge library hearth with its blaze and warmth; and a disreputable fur rug in front of it that might have been ordained expressly for tired dogs to drowse on. And there were the Mistress and the Master. Especially the Mistress! The Mistress somehow had a way of making all the world seem worth while.

Then, of a morning, when Lass was just eleven months old, two things happened.

The Mistress and the Master went down to her kennel after breakfast. Lass did not run forth to greet them as usual. She lay still, wagging her tail in feeble welcome as they drew near. But she did not get up.

Crowding close to her tawny side was a tiny,

shapeless creature that looked more like a fat blind
rat than like anything else. It was a ten-hour-old
collie pup--a male, and yellowish brown of hue.

"That's the climax!" complained the Master,
breaking in on the Mistress's rhapsodies. "Here
we've been planning to start a kennel of home-bred
collies! And see what results we get! One solitary
puppy! Not once in ten times are there less than six
in a collie-litter. Sometimes there are a dozen. And
here the dog you wheedled me into keeping has just
one! I expected at least seven."

"If it's a freak to be the only puppy in a litter,"
answered the Mistress, refusing to part with her
enthusiasm over the miracle, "then this one ought to
bring us luck. Let's call him 'Bruce.' You remember,
the original Bruce won because of the mystic
number, seven. This Bruce has got to make up to us
for the seven puppies that weren't born. See how
proud she is of him! Isn't she a sweet little mother?"

The second of the morning's events was a visit from
the foreman of the Rothsay Kennels, who motored
across to The Place, intent on clearing up a mystery.

"The Boss found a collie yesterday, tied in the front
yard of a negro cabin a mile or two from our
kennels," he told the Master. "He recognized her
right away as Rothsay Princess. The negro claims to
have found her wandering around near the railroad
tracks, one night, six months ago. Now, what's the
answer?"

"The answer," said the Master, "is that your boss is

mistaken. I've had Rothsay Princess for the past six months. And she's the last dog I'll ever get from the Rothsay Kennels. I was stung, good and plenty, on that deal.

"My wife wanted to keep her, or I'd have made a kick in the courts for having to pay two hundred dollars for a cheeky, apple- -domed, prick eared--"

"Prick-eared!" exclaimed the foreman, aghast at the volleyed sacrilege. "Rothsay Princess has the best ears of any pup we've bred since Champion Rothsay Chief. Not a flaw in that pup. She--"

"Not a flaw, hey!" sniffed the Master. "Come down to the kennel and take a look at her. She has as many flaws as a street-cur has fleas."

He led the way to the kennel. At sight of the stranger Lass growled and showed her teeth. For a collie mother will let nobody but proven friends come near to her newborn brood.

The foreman stared at the hostile young mother for a half-minute, whistling bewilderedly between his teeth. Then he laughed aloud.

"That's no more Rothsay Princess than I am!" he declared. "I know who she IS, though. I'd remember that funny mask among a million. That's Rothsay Lass! Though how she got HERE--!

"We couldn't have shipped her by mistake, either," he went on, confused. "For we'd sold her, that same day, to a kid in our town. I ought to know. Because the kid kept on pestering us every day for a month afterward, to find if she had come back to us. He said she ran away in the night. He still comes around, once a week or so, to ask. A spindly, weak, sick-looking little chap, he is. I don't get the point of this thing, from any angle. But we run our kennels on the square. And I can promise the boss'll either send back your check or send Rothsay Princess to you and take Lass back."

Two days later, while all The Place was still mulling over the mystery, a letter came for the Master from Lass's home town. It was signed "Edw'd Hazen," and it was written on the cheap stationery of his employer's bottling works. It read:

Dear Sir:

"Six months ago, my son bought a dog from the Rothsay Kennels. It was a she-dog, and his ma and I didn't want one around. So I put it aboard a freight-car on the sly. My boy went sick over losing his dog. He has never rightly got over it, but he peaks and mopes and gets thinner all the time. If I had known how hard he was going to take it, I would of cut off my hand before I would of done such a thing. And my wife feels just like I do about it. We would both of us have given a hundred dollars to get the dog back for him, when we saw how bad he felt. But it was too late. Somehow or other it is most generally too late when a rotten thing has been done.

"To-day he went again to the Rothsay Kennels to ask if she had come back. He has always been hoping she would. And they told him you have her. Now, sir, I am a poor man, but if one hundred dollars will make you sell me that dog, I'll send it to you in a money order by return mail. It will be worth ten times that much, to my wife and me, to have Dick happy again. I inclose a stamp. Will you let me know?"

Six weeks afterward The Place's car brought Dick Hazen across to receive his long-lost pet.

The boy was thinner and shakier and whiter than when he had gone to sleep with his cherished puppy curled against his narrow chest. But there was a light in his eyes and an eagerness in his heart that had not been there in many a long week.

Lass was on the veranda to welcome him. And as Dick scrambled out of the car and ran to pick her up, she came more than half-way to meet him. With a flurry of fast-pattering steps and a bark of eager welcome, she flung herself upon her long-vanished master. For a highbred collie does not forget. And at first glimpse of the boy Lass remembered him.

Dick caught her up in his arms--a harder feat than of yore, because of her greater weight and his own sapped strength,--and hugged her tight to his breast. Winking very fast indeed to disperse tears that had no place in the eyes of a self-contained man of twelve, he sputtered rapturously:

"I KNEW I'd find you, Lassie--I knew it all the time;--even the times when I was deadsure I wouldn't! Gee, but you've grown, though! And you're beautifuler than ever. Isn't she, Miss?" he demanded, turning to the Mistress with instinctive knowledge that here at least he would find confirmation. "Indeed she is!" the Mistress assured him.

"And see how glad she is to be with you again! She--"

"And Dad says she can stay with me, for keeps!" exulted Dick. "He says he'll put a new lock on the cellar door, so she can't ever push out again, the way she did, last time. But I guess she's had her lesson in going out for walks at night and not being able to find her way back. She and I are going to have the dandiest times together, that ever happened. Aren't we, Lass? Is that her little boy?" he broke off, in eager curiosity, as the Master appeared from the kennels, carrying Bruce.

The puppy was set down on the veranda floor for Dick's inspection.

"He's cunning, isn't he? Kind of like a Teddy Bear,--the sort kids play with. But," with a tinge of worry, "I'm not sure Ma will let me keep two. Maybe--"

"Perhaps," suggested the Mistress, "perhaps you'd like us to keep little Bruce, to remember Lass by? We'll try to make him very happy."

"Yes'm!" agreed Dick, in much haste, his brow clearing from a mental vision of Mrs. Hazen's face when she should see him return with twice as many dogs as he had set out for. "Yes'm. If you wouldn't mind, very much. S'pose we leave it that way? I guess Bruce'll like being with you, Miss. I--I guess pretty near anybody would. You'll--you'll try not to be too homesick for Lass, won't you?"

On the steps of the veranda the downy and fat puppy watched his mother's departure with no especial interest. By the Mistress's wish, Mr. Hazen had not been required to make any part of his proffered hundred-dollar payment for the return of his boy's pet. All the Mistress had stipulated was that Lass might be allowed to remain at The Place until baby Bruce should no longer need her.

"Bruce," said the Mistress as the car rolled up the drive and out of sight, "you are the sole visible result of The Place's experiment in raising prize collies. You have a tremendous responsibility on those fat little shoulders of yours,--to live up to it all."

By way of showing his scorn for such trifles as a "tremendous responsibility," Bruce proceeded to make a ferocious onslaught at the Mistress's temperamental gray Persian kitten, "Tipperary," which was picking a mincing way across the veranda.

A howl of pain and two scratches on his tiny nose immediately followed the attack. Tipperary then went on with her mincing promenade. And Bruce, with loud lamentations, galloped to the shelter of the Mistress's skirt.

"Poor little chap!" soothed the Mistress, picking

him up and comforting him. "Responsibility isn't such a joke, after all, is it, Baby?"

CHAPTER II.

The Pest

Thackeray, as a lad, was dropped from college for laziness and for gambling. Bismarck failed to get a University degree, because he lacked power to study and because he preferred midnight beer to midnight oil. George Washington, in student days, could never grasp the simplest rules of spelling. The young Lincoln loved to sprawl in the shade with fish-pole or tattered book, when he should have been working.

Now, these men were giants--physically as well as mentally. Being giants, they were by nature slow of development.

The kitten, at six months of age, is graceful and compact and of perfect poise. The lion-cub, at the same age, is a gawky and foolish and ill-knit mass of legs and fur; deficient in sense and in symmetry. Yet at six years, the lion and the cat are not to be compared for power or beauty or majesty or brain, or along any other lines.

The foregoing is not an essay on the slow development of the Great. It is merely a condensation of the Mistress's earnest arguments

against the selling or giving away of a certain
hopelessly awkward and senseless and altogether
undesirable collie pup named Bruce.

From the very first, the Mistress had been Bruce's
champion at The Place. There was no competition
for that office. She and she alone could see any
promise in the shambling youngster.

Because he had been born on The Place, and
because he was the only son of Rothsay Lass,
whom, the Mistress had also championed against
strong opposition, it had been decided to keep and
raise him. But daily this decision seemed less and
less worth while. Only the Mistress's championing
of the Undesirable prevented his early banishment.

From a fuzzy and adventurous fluff-ball of gray-
gold-and-white fur, Bruce swiftly developed into a
lanky giant. He was almost as large again as is the
average collie pup of his age; but, big as he was, his
legs and feet and head were huge, out of all
proportion to the rest of him. The head did not
bother him. Being hampered by no weight of brain,
it would be navigated with more or less ease, in
spite of its bulk. But the legs and feet were not only
in his own way, but in every one else's.

He seemed totally lacking in sense, as well as in
bodily coordination. He was forever getting into
needless trouble. He was a stormcenter. No one but
a born fool--canine or human--could possibly have
caused one-tenth as much bother.

The Mistress had named him "Bruce," after the

stately Scottish chieftain who was her history-hero. And she still called him Bruce--fifty times a day--in the weary hope of teaching him his name. But every one else on The Place gave him a title instead of a name--a title that stuck: "The Pest." He spent twenty-four hours, daily, living up to it.

Compared with Bruce's helplessly clownish trouble-seeking propensities, Charlie Chaplin's screen exploits are miracles of heroic dignity and of good luck.

There was a little artificial water-lily pool on The Place, perhaps four feet deep. By actual count, Bruce fell into it no less than nine times in a single week. Once or twice he had nearly drowned there before some member of the family chanced to fish him out. And, learning nothing from experience, he would fall in again, promptly, the next day.

The Master at last rigged up a sort of sloping wooden platform, running from the lip of the pool into the water, so that Bruce could crawl out easily, next time he should tumble in. Bruce watched the placing of this platform with much grave interest. The moment it was completed, he trotted down it on a tour of investigation. At its lower edge he slipped and rolled into the pool. There he floundered, with no thought at all of climbing out as he had got in, until the Master rescued him and spread a wire net over the whole pool to avert future accidents.

Thenceforth, Bruce met with no worse mischance, there, than the - perpetual catching of his toe-pads in the meshes of the wire. Thus ensnared he would

stand, howling most lamentably, until his yells
brought rescue.

Though the pool could be covered with a net, the
wide lake at the foot of the lawn could not be. Into
the lake Bruce would wade till the water reached
his shoulders. Then with a squeal of venturesome
joy, he would launch himself outward for a swim;
and, once facing away from shore, he never had
sense enough to turn around.

After a half-hour of steady swimming, his soft
young strength would collapse. A howl of terror
would apprise the world at large that he was about
to drown. Whereat some passing boatman would
pick him up and hold him for ransom, or else some
one from The Place must jump into skiff or canoe
and hie with all speed to the rescue. The same thing
would be repeated day after day.

The local S.P.C.A. threatened to bring action
against the Master for letting his dog risk death, in
this way, from drowning. Morbidly, the Master
wished the risk might verge into a certainty.

The puppy's ravenous appetite was the wonder of
all. He stopped eating only when there was nothing
edible in reach. And as his ideas of edible food
embraced everything that was chewable,--from
bath-towels to axle-grease--he was seldom fasting
and was frequently ill.

Nature does more for animals than for humans. By a
single experience she warns them, as a rule, what
they may safely eat and what they may not. Bruce

was the exception. He would pounce upon and
devour a luscious bit of laundry-soap with just as
much relish as though a similar bit of soap had not
made him horribly sick the day before.

Once he munched, relishfully, a two-pound box of
starch, box and all; on his recovery, he began upon
a second box, and was unhappy when it was taken
from him.

He would greet members of the family with
falsetto-thunderous barks of challenge as they came
down the drive from the highway. But he would
frisk out in joyous welcome to meet and fawn upon
tramps or peddlers who sought to invade The Place.
He could scarce learn his own name. He could
hardly be taught to obey the simplest command. As
for shaking hands or lying down at order (those two
earliest bits of any dog's education), they meant no
more to Bruce than did the theory of quadratic
equations.

At three months he launched forth merrily as a
chicken-killer; gleefully running down and
beheading The Place's biggest Orpington rooster.
But his first kill was his last. The Master saw to
that.

There is no use in thrashing a dog for killing
poultry. There is but one practically sure cure for
the habit. And this one cure the Master applied.

He tied the slain rooster firmly around Bruce's furry
throat, and made the puppy wear it, as a heavy and
increasingly malodorous pendant, for three warm

days and nights.

Before the end of this seventy-two-hour period, Bruce had grown to loathe the sight and scent of chicken. Stupid as he was, he learned this lesson with absolute thoroughness,--as will almost any chicken-killing pup,--and it seemed to be the only teaching that his unawakened young brain had the power to grasp.

In looks, too, Bruce was a failure. His yellowish-and-white body was all but shapeless. His coat was thick and heavy enough, but it showed a tendency to curl--almost to kink--instead of waving crisply, as a collie's ought. The head was coarse and blurred in line. The body was gaunt, in spite of its incessant feedings. As for contour or style--

It was when the Master, in disgust, pointed out these diverse failings of the pup, that the Mistress was wont to draw on historic precedent for other instances of slow development, and to take in vain the names of Thackeray, Lincoln, Washington and Bismarck and the rest.

"Give him time!" she urged once. "He isn't quite six months old yet; and he has grown so terribly fast. Why, he's over two feet tall, at the shoulder, even now--much bigger than most full-grown collies. Champion Howgill Rival is spoken of as a 'big' dog; yet he is only twenty-four inches at the shoulder, Mr. Leighton says. Surely it's something to own a dog that is so big."

"It IS 'something,'" gloomily conceded the Master.

"In our case it is a catastrophe. I don't set up to be an expert judge of collies, so maybe I am all wrong about him. I'm going to get professional opinion, though. Next week they are going to have the spring dogshow at Hampton. It's a little hole-in-a-corner show, of course. But Symonds is to be the all-around judge, except for the toy breeds. And Symonds knows collies, from the ground up. I am going to take Bruce over there and enter him for the puppy class. If he is any good, Symonds will know it. If the dog is as worthless as I think he is, I'll get rid of him. If Symonds gives any hope for him, I'll keep him on a while longer."

"But," ventured the Mistress, "if Symonds says 'Thumbs down,' then--"

"Then I'll buy a pet armadillo or an ornithorhynchus instead," threatened the Master. "Either of them will look more like a collie than Bruce does."

"I--I wonder if Mr. Symonds smokes," mused the Mistress under her breath.

"Smokes?" echoed the Master. "What's that got to do with it?"

"I was only wondering," she made hesitant answer, "if a box of very wonderful cigars, sent to him with our cards, mightn't perhaps--"

"It's a fine sportsmanly proposition!" laughed the Master. "When women get to ruling the world of sport, there'll be no need of comic cartoons. Genuine photographs will do as well. If it's just the same to you, dear girl, we'll let Symonds buy his own cigars, for the present. The dog-show game is almost the only one I know of where a judge is practically always on the square. People doubt his judgment, sometimes, but there is practically never any doubt of his honesty. Besides, we want to get the exact dope on Bruce. (Not that I haven't got it, already!) If Symonds 'gates' him, I'm going to offer him for sale at the show. If nobody buys him there, I'm going--"

"He hasn't been 'gated' yet," answered the Mistress in calm confidence.

At the little spring show, at Hampton, a meager eighty dogs were exhibited, of which only nine were collies. This collie division contained no specimens to startle the dog-world. Most of the exhibits were pets. And like nearly all pets, they were "seconds"--in other words, the less desirable dogs of thoroughbred litters.

Hampton's town hall auditorium was filled to overcrowding, with a mass of visitors who paraded interestedly along the aisles between the raised rows of stall-like benches where the dogs were tied; or who grouped densely around all four sides of the roped judging-ring in the center of the hall.

For a dogshow has a wel-nigh universal appeal to humanity at large; even as the love for dogs is one of the primal and firm- rooted human emotions. Not only the actual exhibitor and their countless friends flock to such shows; but the public at large is drawn thither as to no other function of the kind.

Horse-racing, it is true, brings out a crowd many times larger than does a dogshow. But only because of the thrill of winning or losing money. For where one's spare cash is, there is his heart and his all-absorbing interest. Yet it is a matter of record that grass is growing high, on the race-tracks, in such states as have been able to enforce the anti-betting laws. The "sport of kings" flourishes only where wagers may accompany it. Remove the betting element, and you turn your racetrack into a huge and untrodden lot.

There is practically no betting connected with any dogshow. People go there to see the dogs and to watch their judging, and for nothing else. As a rule, the show is not even a social event. Nevertheless, the average dogshow is thronged with spectators. (Try to cross Madison Square Garden, on Washington's Birthday afternoon, while the Westminster Kennel Club's Show is in progress. If you can work your way through the press of visitors in less than half an hour, then Nature intended you for a football champion.)

The fortunate absence of a betting-interest alone keeps such affairs from becoming among the foremost sporting features of the world. Many of the dogs on view are fools, of course. Because many of them have been bred solely with a view to show-points. And their owners and handlers have done nothing to awaken in their exhibits the half-human brain and heart that is a dog's heritage. All has been sacrificed to "points"--to points which are arbitrary and which change as freakily as do fashions in dress.

For example, a few years ago, a financial giant collected and exhibited one of the finest bunches of collies on earth. He had a competent manager and an army of kennel-men to handle them. He took inordinate pride in these priceless collies of his. Once I watched him, at the Garden Show, displaying them to some Wall Street friends. Three times he made errors in naming his dogs. Once, when he leaned too close to the star collie of his kennels, the dog mistook him for a stranger and resented the intrusion by snapping at him. He did not know his own pets, one from another. And they did not know their owner, by sight or by scent.

At the small shows, there is an atmosphere wholly different. Few of the big breeders bother to compete at such contests. The dogs are for the most part pets, for which their owners feel a keen personal affection, and which have been brought up as members of their masters' households. Thus, if small shows seldom bring forth a world-beating dog, they at least are full of clever and humanized exhibits and of men and women to whom the success or failure of their canine friends is a matter of intensest personal moment. Wherefore the small show often gives the beholder something he can find but rarely in a larger exhibition.

A few dogs genuinely enjoy shows--or are supposed to. To many others a dogshow is a horror.

Which windy digression brings us back by prosy degrees to Bruce and to the Hampton dogshow.

The collies were the first breed to be judged. And

the puppy class, as usual, was the first to be called
to the ring.

There were but three collie pups, all males. One was
a rangy tri- color of eleven months, with a fair head
and a bad coat. The second was an exquisite six-
months puppy, rich of coat, prematurely perfect of
head, and cowhocked. These two and Bruce formed
the puppy class which paraded before Symonds in
the oblong ring.

"Anyhow," whispered the Mistress as the Master
led his stolidly gigantic entry toward the enclosure,
"Bruce can't get worse than a third-prize yellow
ribbon. We ought to be a little proud of that. There
are only three entries in his class."

But even that bit of barren pride was denied the
awkward youngster's sponsor. As the three pups
entered the enclosure. the judge's half-shut eyes
rested on Bruce--at first idly, then in real
amazement. Crossing to the Master, before giving
the signal for the first maneuvers, he said in tired
disgust--

"Please take your measly St. Bernard monstrosity
out of the ring. This is a class for collies, not for
freaks. I refuse to judge that pup as a collie."

"He's a thoroughbred," crossly protested the Master.
"I have his certified pedigree. There's no better
blood in--"

"I don't care what his ancestors were," snapped the
judge. "He's a throw-back to the dinosaur or the

Great Auk. And I won't judge him as a collie. Take him out of the ring. You're delaying the others."

A judge's decision is final. Red with angry shame and suppressing an unworthy desire to kick the luckless Bruce, the Master led the pup back to his allotted bench. Bruce trotted cheerily along with a maddening air of having done something to be proud of. Deaf to the Mistress's sympathy and to her timidly voiced protests, the Master scrawled on an envelope-back the words "For Sale. Name Your Own Price," and pinned it on the edge of the bench.

"Here endeth the first lesson in collie-raising, so far as The Place is concerned," he decreed, stalking back to the ringside to watch the rest of the judging.

The Mistress lingered behind, to bestow a furtive consolatory pat upon the disqualified Bruce. Then she joined her husband beside the ring.

It was probably by accident that her skirt brushed sharply against the bench-edge as she went-- knocking the "For Sale" sign down into the litter of straw below.

But a well-meaning fellow-exhibitor, across the aisle, saw the bit of paper flutter floorward. This good soul rescued it from the straw and pinned it back in place.

(The world is full of helpful folk. That is perhaps one reason why the Millennium's date is still so indefinite.)

An hour later, a man touched the Master on the arm.

"That dog of your, on Bench 48," began the stranger, "the big pup with the 'For Sale' sign on his bench. What do you want for him?"

The Mistress was several feet away, talking to the superintendent of the show. Guiltily, yet gratefully, the Master led the would- be purchaser back to the benches, without attracting his wife's notice.

A few minutes afterward he returned to where she and the superintendent were chatting.

"Well," said the Master, trying to steel himself against his wife's possible disappointment, "I found a buyer for Bruce--a Dr. Halding, from New York. He likes the pup. Says Bruce looks as if he was strong and had lots of endurance. I wonder if he wants him for a sledge-dog. He paid me fifteen dollars for him; and it was a mighty good bargain. I was lucky to get more than a nickel for such a cur."

The Master shot forth this speech in almost a single rapid breath. Then, before his wife could reply,-- and without daring to look into her troubled eyes,-- he discovered an acquaintance on the far side of the ring and bustled off to speak to him. The Master, you see, was a husband, not a hero.

The Mistress turned a worried gaze on the superintendent.

"It was best, I suppose," she said bravely. "We agreed he must be sold, if the judge decided he was not any good. But I'm sorry. For I'm fond of him. I'm sorry he is going to live in New York, too. A big city is no place for a big dog. I hope this Dr. Halding will be nice to the poor puppy."

"Dr.--WHO?" sharply queried the superintendent, who had not caught the name when the Master had spoken it in his rapid-fire speech. "Dr. Halding? Of New York? Huh!

"You needn't worry about the effect of city life on your dog," he went on with venomous bitterness. "The pup won't have a very long spell of it. If I had my way, that man Halding would be barred from every dog-show and stuck in jail. It's an old trick of his, to buy up thoroughbreds, cheap, at shows. The bigger and the stronger they are, the more he pays for them. He seems to think pedigreed dogs are better for his filthy purposes than street curs. They have a higher nervous organism, I suppose. The swine!"

"What do you mean?" asked the Mistress, puzzled by his vehemence. "I don't--"

"You must have heard of Halding and his so-called 'research work,'" the superintendent went on. "He is one of the most notorious vivisectionists in--"

The superintendent got no further. He was talking to empty air. The Mistress had fled. Her determined small figure made a tumbled wake through the crowd as she sped toward Bruce's bench. The puppy was no longer there. In another second the Mistress was at the door of the building.

A line of parked cars was stretched across the opposite side of the village street. Into one of these cars a large and loose- jointed man was lifting a large and loose-jointed dog. The dog did not like his treatment, and was struggling pathetically in vain awkwardness to get free.

"Bruce!" called the Mistress, fiercely, as she dashed across the street.

The puppy heard the familiar voice and howled for release. Dr. Halding struck him roughly over the head and scrambled into the machine with him, reaching with his one disengaged hand for the self-starter button. Before he could touch it, the Mistress was on the running-board of the car.

As she ran, she had opened her wristbag. Now, flinging on the runabout's seat a ten and a five-dollar bill, she demanded--

"Give me my dog! There is the money you paid for him!"

"He isn't for sale," grinned the Doctor. "Stand clear, please. I'm starting."

"You're doing nothing of the sort," was the hot reply. "You'll give back my dog! Do you understand?"

For answer Halding reached again toward his self-starter. A renewed struggle from the whimpering puppy frustrated his aim and forced him to devote both hands to the subduing of Bruce. The dog was making frantic writhings to get to the Mistress. She caught his furry ruff and raged on, sick with anger

"I know who you are and what you want this poor frightened puppy for. You shan't have him! There seems to be no law to prevent human devils from strapping helpless dogs to a table and torturing them to death in the unholy name of science. But if there isn't a corner waiting for them, below, it's only because Hades can't be made hot enough to punish such men as they ought to be punished! You're not going to torture Bruce. There's your money. Let go of him."

"You talk like all silly, sloppy sentimentalists!" scoffed the Doctor, his slight German accent becoming more noticeable as he continued: "A woman can't have the intellect to understand our services to humanity. We--"

"Neither have half the real doctors!" she flashed. "Fully half of them deny that vivisection ever helped humanity. And half the remainder say they are in doubt. They can't point to a single definite case where it has been of use. Alienists say it's a distinct form of mental perversion,--the craving to torture dumb animals to death and to make scientific notes of their sufferings."

"Pah!" he sniffed. "I--"

She hurried on

"If humanity can't be helped without cutting live dogs and kittens to shreds, in slow agony--then so much the worse for humanity! If you vivisectors would be content to practice on one another--or on condemned murderers,--instead of on friendly and innocent dogs, there'd be no complaint from any one. But leave our pets alone. Let go of my puppy!"

By way of response the Doctor grunted in lofty contempt. At the same time he tucked the wriggling dog under his right arm, holding him thus momentarily safe, and pressed the self-starter button.

There was a subdued whir. A move of Halding's foot and a release of the brake, and the car started forward.

"Stand clear!" he ordered. "I'm going."

The jolt of the sudden start was too much for the Mistress's balance on the running-board. Back she toppled. Only by luck did she land on her feet instead of her head, upon the greasy pavement of the street.

But she sprang forward again, with a little cry of indignant dismay, and reached desperately into the moving car for Bruce, calling him eagerly by name.

Dr. Halding was steering with his left hand, while his viselike right arm still encircled the protesting collie. As the Mistress ran alongside and grasped frantically for her doomed pet, he let go of Bruce for an instant, to fend off her hand--or perhaps to thrust her away from the peril of the fast-moving mud-guards. At the Mistress's cry--and at the brief letup of pressure caused by the Doctor's menacing gesture toward the unhappy woman--Bruce's long-sleeping soul awoke. He answered the cry and the man's blow at his deity in the immemorial fashion of all dogs whose human gods are threatened.

There was a snarling wild-beast growl, the first that ever had come from the clownlike puppy's throat,--and Bruce flung his unwieldy young body straight for the vivisector's throat.

Halding, with a vicious fist-lunge, sent the pup to the floor of the car in a crumpled heap, but not before the curving white eyeteeth had slashed the side of the man's throat in an ugly flesh-wound that drove its way dangerously close to the jugular.

Half stunned by the blow, and with the breath knocked out of him, Bruce none the less gathered himself together with lightning speed and launched his bulk once more for Halding's throat.

This time he missed his mark--for several things happened all at once.

At the dog's first onslaught, Halding's foot had swung forward, along with his fist, in an instinctive kick. The kick did not reach Bruce. But it landed, full and effectively, on the accelerator.

The powerful car responded to the touch with a bound. And it did so at the very moment that the flash of white teeth at his throat made Halding snatch his own left hand instinctively from the steering-wheel, in order to guard the threatened spot.

A second later the runabout crashed at full speed into the wall of a house on the narrow street's opposite side.

The rest was chaos.

When a crowd of idlers and a policeman at last righted the wrecked car, two bodies were found huddled inertly amid a junk- heap of splintered glass and shivered wood and twisted metal. The local ambulance carried away one of these limp bodies. The Place's car rushed the smash-up's other senseless victim to the office of the nearest veterinary. Dr. Halding, with a shattered shoulder-blade and a fractured nose and jaw and a mild case of brain-concussion,--was received as a guest of honor at the village hospital.

Bruce, his left foreleg broken and a nasty assortment of glass- cuts marring the fluffiness of his fur, was skillfully patched up by the vet' and carried back that night to The Place.

The puppy had suddenly taken on a new value in his owners' eyes-- partly for his gallantly puny effort at defending the Mistress, partly because of his pitiful condition. And he was nursed, right zealously, back to life and health.

In a few weeks, the plaster cast on the convalescent's broken foreleg had been replaced by a bandage. In another week or two the vet' pronounced Bruce as well as ever. The dog, through habit, still held the mended foreleg off the ground, even after the bandage was removed. Whereat, the Master tied a bandage tightly about the uninjured foreleg.

Bruce at once decided that this, and not the other, was the lame leg; and he began forthwith to limp on it. As it was manifestly impossible to keep both forelegs off the ground at the same time when he was walking, he was forced to make use of the once-broken leg. Finding, to his amaze, that he could walk on it with perfect ease, he devoted his limping solely to the well leg. And as soon as the Master took the bandage from that, Bruce ceased to limp at all.

Meanwhile, a lawyer, whose name sounded as though it had been culled from a Rhine Wine list, had begun suit, in Dr. Halding's name, against the Mistress, as a "contributory cause" of his client's accident. The suit never came to trial. It was dropped, indeed, with much haste. Not from any change of heart on the plaintiff's behalf; but because, at that juncture, Dr. Halding chanced to be arrested and interned as a dangerous Enemy Alien. Our country had recently declared war on Germany; and the belated spy-hunt was up.

During the Federal officers' search of the doctor's house, for treasonable documents (of which they found an ample supply), they came upon his laboratory. No fewer than five dogs, in varying stages of hideous torture, were found strapped to tables or hanging to wall-hooks. The vivisector bewailed, loudly and gutturally, this cruel interruption to his researches in Science's behalf.

One day, two months after the accident, Bruce stood on all four feet once more, with no vestige left of scars or of lameness. And then, for the first time, a steady change that had been so slow as to escape any one's notice dawned upon the Mistress and the Master. It struck them both at the same moment. And they stared dully at their pet.

The shapeless, bumptious, foolish Pest of two months ago had vanished. In his place, by a very normal process of nature-magic, stood a magnificently stately thoroughbred collie.

The big head had tapered symmetrically, and had lost its puppy formlessness. It was now a head worthy of Landseer's own pencil. The bonily awkward body had lengthened and had lost its myriad knobs and angles. It had grown massively graceful.

The former thatch of half-curly and indeterminately yellowish fuzz had changed to a rough tawny coat, wavy and unbelievably heavy, stippled at the ends with glossy black. There was a strange depth and repose and Soul in the dark eyes--yes, and a keen intelligence, too.

It was the old story of the Ugly Duckling, all over again.

"Why!" gasped the Mistress. "He's--he's BEAUTIFUL! And I never knew it."

At her loved voice the great dog moved across to where she sat. Lightly he laid one little white paw on her knee and looked gravely up into her eyes.

"He's got sense, too," chimed in the Master. "Look at those eyes, if you doubt it. They're alive with intelligence. It's--it's a miracle! He can't be the same worthless whelp I wanted to get rid of! He CAN'T!"

And he was not. The long illness, at the most formative time of the dog's growth, had done its work in developing what, all the time, had lain latent. The same illness--and the long-enforced personal touch with humans--had done an equally transforming work on the puppy's undeveloped mind. The Thackeray-Washington- Lincoln- Bismarck simile had held good.

What looked like a miracle was no more than the same beautifully simple process which Nature enacts every day, when she changes an awkward and dirt-colored cygnet into a glorious swan or a leggily gawky colt into a superb Derby-winner. But Bruce's metamorphosis seemed none the less wonderful in the eyes of the two people who had learned to love him.

Somewhere in the hideous wreck of Dr. Halding's motorcar the dog had found a soul--and the rest had followed as a natural course of growth.

At the autumn dog-show, in Hampton, a "dark-sable-and-white" collie of unwonted size and beauty walked proudly into the ring close to the Mistress's side, when the puppy class was called--a class that includes all dogs under twelve months old. Six minutes later the Mistress was gleesomely accepting the first-prize blue ribbon, for "best puppy," from Judge Symonds' own gnarled hand.

Then came the other classes for collies--"Novice," "Open," "Limit," "Local," "American Bred." And as Bruce paced majestically out of the ring at last, he was the possessor of five more blue ribbons--as well as the blue Winner's rosette, for "best collie in the show."

"Great dog you've got there, madam!" commented Symonds in solemn approval as he handed the Winner's rosette to the Mistress. "Fine dog in every way. Fine promise. He will go far. One of the best types I've--"

"Do you really think so?" sweetly replied the Mistress. "Why, one of the foremost collie judges in America has gone on record as calling him a 'measly St. Bernard monstrosity.'"

"No?" snorted Symonds, incredulous. "You don't say so! A judge who would speak so, of that dog, doesn't understand his business. He--"

"Oh, yes, he does!" contradicted the Mistress, glancing lovingly at her handful of blue ribbons. "I think he understands his business very well indeed--NOW!"

CHAPTER III.

The War Dog

The guest had decided to wait until next morning, before leaving The Place, instead of following his first plan of taking a night train to New York. He was a captain in our regular army and had newly come back from France to forget an assortment of shrapnel-- bites and to teach practical tactics to rookies.

He reached his decision to remain over night at The Place while he and the Mistress and the Master were sitting on the vine-hung west veranda after dinner, watching the flood of sunset change the lake to molten gold and the sky to pink fire. It would be pleasant to steal another few hours at this back-country House of Peace before returning to the humdrum duties of camp. And the guest yielded to the temptation.

"I'm mighty glad you can stay over till morning," said the Master. "I'll send word to Roberts not to bring up the car."

As he spoke, he scrawled a penciled line on an envelope-back; then he whistled.

From a cool lounging-place beneath the wistaria-vines arose a huge collie--stately of form, dark brown and white of coat, deep- set of eye and with a head that somehow reminded one of a Landseer engraving. The collie trotted up the steps of the veranda and stood expectant before the Master. The latter had been folding the envelope lengthwise. Now he slipped it through the ring in the dog's collar.

"Give it to Roberts," he said.

The big collie turned and set off at a hand-gallop.

"Good!" approved the guest. "Bruce didn't seem to be in any doubt as to what you wanted him to do. He knows where Roberts is likely to be?"

"No," said the Master. "But he can track him and find him, if Roberts is anywhere within a mile or so from here. That was one of the first things we taught him--to carry messages. All we do is to slip the paper into his collar-ring and tell him the name of the person to take it to. Naturally, he knows us all by name. So it is easy enough for him to do it. We look on the trick as tremendously clever. But that's because we love Bruce. Almost any dog can be taught to do it, I suppose. We--"

"You're mistaken!" corrected the guest. "Almost any dog CAN'T be taught to. Some dogs can, of course; but they are the exception. I ought to know, for I've been where dog-couriers are a decidedly important feature of trench-warfare. I stopped at one of the dog- training schools in England, too, on my way back from Picardy, and watched the teaching of the dogs that are sent to France and Flanders. Not one in ten can be trained to carry messages; and not one in thirty can be counted on to do it reliably. You ought to be proud of Bruce."

"We are," replied the Mistress. "He is one of the family. We think everything of him. He was such a stupid and awkward puppy, too! Then, in just a few months, he shaped up, as he is now. And his brain woke."

Bruce interrupted the talk by reappearing on the veranda. The folded envelope was still in the ring on his collar. The guest glanced furtively at the Master, expecting some sign of chagrin at the collie's failure.

Instead, the Master took the envelope, unfolded it and glanced at a word or two that had been written beneath his own scrawl; then he made another penciled addition to the envelope's writing, stuck the twisted paper back into the ring and said--

"Roberts."

Off trotted Bruce on his second trip.

"I had forgotten to say which train you'll have to take in the morning," explained the Master. "So Roberts wrote, asking what time he was to have the car at the door after breakfast. It was careless of me."

The guest did not answer. But when Bruce presently returned,-- this time with no paper in his collar-ring,--the officer passed his hand appraisingly through the dog's heavy coat and looked keenly down into his dark eyes.

"Gun-shy?" asked the guest. "Or perhaps he's never

heard a gun fired?"

"He's heard hundreds of guns fired," said the Master. "I never allow a gun to be fired on The Place, of course, because we've made it a bird refuge. But Bruce went with us in the car to the testing of the Lewis machineguns, up at Haskell. They made a most ungodly racket. But somehow it didn't seem to bother the Big Dog at all."

"H'm!" mused the guest, his professional interest vehemently roused. "He would be worth a fortune over there. There are a lot of collies in the service, in one capacity or another--almost as many as the Airedales and the police dogs. And they are doing grand work. But I never saw one that was better fitted for it than Bruce. It's a pity he lives on the wrong side of the Atlantic. He could do his bit, to more effect than the average human. There are hundreds of thousands of men for the ranks, but pitifully few perfect courier-dogs."

The Mistress was listening with a tensity which momentarily grew more painful. The Master's forehead, too, was creased with a new thought that seemed to hurt him. To break the brief silence that followed the guest's words, he asked:

"Are the dogs, over there, really doing such great work as the papers say they are? I read, the other day--"

" 'Great work!'" repeated the guest. "I should say so. Not only in finding the wounded and acting as guards on listening posts, and all that, but most of all as couriers. There are plenty of times when the wireless can't be used for sending messages from one point to another, and where there is no telephone connection, and where the firing is too hot for a human courier to get through. That is where is the war dogs have proved their weight in radium. Collies, mostly. There are a, million true stories of their prowess told, at camp-fires. Here are just two such incidents--both of them on record, by the way, at the British War Office

"A collie, down near Soissons, was sent across a bad strip of fire-scourged ground, with a message. A boche sharpshooter fired at him and shattered his jaw. The dog kept on, in horrible agony, and delivered the message. Another collie was sent over a still hotter and much longer stretch of territory with a message. (That was during the Somme drive of 1916.) He was shot at, a dozen times, as he ran. At last two bullets got him. He fell over, mortally wounded. He scrambled to his feet and kept on falling, stumbling, staggering--till he got to his destination. Then he dropped dead at the side of the Colonel the message had been sent to. And those are only two of thousands of true collie-anecdotes. Yet some fools are trying to get American dogs done away with, as 'non-utilitarian,' while the war lasts! As if the dogs in France, today, weren't earning their overseas brothers' right to live-- and live well!"

Neither of his hearers made reply when the guest finished his earnest, eager recital. Neither of them had paid much heed to his final words. For the Master and the Mistress were looking at each other in mute unhappiness. The same miserable thought was in the mind of each. And each knew the thought that was torturing the mind of the other.

Presently, at a glint of inquiry in the Master's eye, the Mistress suddenly bent over and buried her face in the deep mass of Bruce's ruff as the dog stood lovingly beside her. Then, still stroking the collie's silken head, she returned her husband's wretchedly questioning glance with a resigned little nod. The Master cleared his throat noisily before he could speak with the calm indifference he sought. Then, turning to the apparently unnoticing guest, he said--

"I think I told you I tried to get across to France at the very start--and I was barred because I am past forty and because I have a bum heart and several other defects that a soldier isn't supposed to have. My wife and I have tried to do what little we can for the Cause, on this side of the ocean. But it has seemed woefully little, when we remember what others are doing. And we have no son we can send."

Again he cleared his throat and went on with sulky ungraciousness:

"We both know what you've been driving at for the past five minutes. And--and we agree. Bruce can go."

"Great!" applauded the guest. "That's fine! He'll be worth his--"

"If you think we're a couple of fools for not doing this more willingly," went on the Master with

savage earnestness, "just stop to think what it means
to a man to give up the dog he loves. Not to give
him up to some one who will assure him a good
home, but to send him over into that hell, where a
German bullet or a shell-fragment or hunger or
disease is certain to get him, soon or late. To think
of him lying smashed and helpless, somewhere in
No Man's Land, waiting for death; or caught by the
enemy and eaten! (The Red Cross bulletin says no
less than eight thousand dogs were eaten, in Saxony
alone, in 1913, the year BEFORE the war began.)
Or else to be captured and then cut up by some
German vivisector-surgeon in the sacred interests of
Science! Oh, we can bring ourselves to send Bruce
over there! But don't expect us to do it with a good
grace. For we can't."

"I--" began the embarrassed guest; but the Mistress
chimed in, her sweet voice not quite steady.

"You see, Captain, we've made such a pet--such a
baby--of Bruce! All his life he has lived here--here
where he had the woods to wander in and the lake
to swim in, and this house for his home. He will be
so unhappy and--Well, don't let's talk about that!
When I think of the people who give their sons and
everything they have, to the country, I feel ashamed
of not being more willing to let a mere dog go. But
then Bruce is not just a 'mere dog.' He is--he is
BRUCE. All I ask is that if he is injured and not
killed, you'll arrange to have him sent back here to
us. We'll pay for it, of course. And will you write to
whomever you happen to know, at that dog-training
school in England, and ask that Bruce be treated
nicely while he is training there? He's never been

whipped. He's never needed it, you see."

The Mistress might have spared herself much worry as to Bruce's treatment in the training school to which he was consigned. It was not a place of cruelty, but of development. And when, out of the thousands of dogs sent there, the corps of trainers found one with promise of strong ability, such a pupil was handled with all the care and gentleness and skill that a temperamental prima donna might expect.

Such a dog was the big American collie, debarked from a goods car at the training camp railway station, six weeks after the Mistress and the Master had consented to his enlistment. And the handlers treated him accordingly.

The Master himself had taken Bruce to the transport, in Brooklyn, and had led him aboard the overfull ship. The new sights and sounds around him interested the home-bred collie. But when the Master turned him over to the officer in whose charge he was to be for the voyage, Bruce's deep-set eyes clouded with a sudden heartsick foreboding.

Wrenching himself free from the friendly hand on his collar, he sprang in pursuit of his departing deity,--the loved Master who was leaving him alone and desolate among all these strange scenes and noises. The Master, plodding, sullen and heavy-hearted, toward the gangway, was aware of a cold nose thrust into his dejected hand.

Looking down he beheld Bruce staring up at him

with a world of stark appeal in his troubled gaze.
The Master swallowed hard; then laid his hand on
the beautiful head pressed so confidingly against his
knee. Turning, he led the dog back to the quarters
assigned to him.

"Stay here, old friend!" he commanded, huskily.
"It's all right. You'll make good. I know that. And
there's a chance in a billion that you'll come back to
us. I'm--I'm not deserting you. And I guess there's
precious little danger that any one on The Place will
ever forget you. It's--it's all right. Millions of
humans are doing it. I'd give everything I've got, if I
could go, too. IT'S ALL RIGHT!"

Then Bruce understood at last that he was to stay in
this place of abominations, far from everything he
loved; and that he must do so because the Master
ordained it. He made no further effort to break away
and to follow his god ashore. But he shivered
convulsively from head to foot; and his desolate
gaze continued to trace the Master's receding figure
out of sight. Then, with a long sigh, he lay down,
heavily, his head between his white forepaws, and
resigned himself to whatever of future misery his
deities might have ordained for him.

Ensued a fortnight of mental and bodily anguish, as
the inland- reared dog tasted the horrors of a voyage
in a rolling ship, through heaving seas. Afterward,
came the landing at a British port and the train ride
to the camp which was to be his home for the next
three months.

Bruce's sense of smell told him the camp contained

more dogs than ever he had beheld in all his brief life put together. But his hearing would have led him to believe there were not a dozen other dogs within a mile of him.

From the encampment arose none of the rackety barking which betokens the presence of many canines, and which deafens visitors to a dog-show.

One of the camp's first and most stringent rules forbade barking, except under special order. These dogs--or the pick of them--were destined for work at the front. The bark of a dog has a carrying quality greater than the combined shouting of ten men. It is the last sound to follow a balloonist, after he has risen above the reach of all other earth-noises.

Hence, a chance bark, rising through the night to where some enemy airman soared with engines turned off, might well lead to the bombing of hitherto unlocated trenches or detachment-camps. For this and divers other reasons, the first lesson taught to arriving wardogs was to abstain from barking.

The dogs were divided, roughly, by breeds, as regarded the line of training assigned to them. The collies were taught courier- work. The Airedales, too,--hideous, cruel, snake-headed,--were used as couriers, as well as to bear Red Cross supplies and to hunt for the wounded. The gaunt and wolflike police dogs were pressed into the two latter tasks, and were taught listening-post duty. And so on through all available breeds,--including the stolidly wise Old English sheepdogs who were to prove invaluable in finding and succoring and reporting the wounded,--down to the humble terriers and mongrels who were taught to rid trenches of vermin.

Everywhere was quiet efficiency and tirelessly patient and skillful work on the part of the trainers. For Britain's best dog men had been recruited for service here. On the perfection of their charges' training might depend the fate of many thousand gallant soldiers. Wherefore, the training was perfect.

Hundreds of dogs proved stupid or unreliable or gun-shy or too easily confused in moments of stress. These were weeded out, continually, and shipped back to the masters who had proffered them.

Others developed with amazing speed and cleverness, grasping their profession as could few human soldiers. And Bruce, lonely and heartsore, yet throwing himself into his labors with all the zest of the best thoroughbred type,--was one of this group.

His early teachings now stood him in good stead. What once had been a jolly game, for his own amusement and that of the Mistress and the Master, was now his life-work. Steadily his trainer wrought over him, bringing out latent abilities that would have dumfounded his earliest teachers, steadying and directing the gayly dashing intelligence; upbuilding and rounding out all his native gifts.

A dog of Bruce's rare type made up to the trainers
for the dullness of their average pupils. He learned
with bewildering ease. He never forgot a lesson
once taught.

No, the Mistress need not have interceded to save
him from beating. As soon would an impresario
think of thrashing Caruso or

Paderewski as would Bruce's glum Scottish trainer
have laid whip to this best pupil of his. Life was
bare and strict for Bruce. But life was never unkind
to him, in these first months of exile from The
Place. And, bit by bit, he began to take a joy in his
work.

Not for a day,--perhaps not for an hour, did the big
collie forget the home of his babyhood or those he
had delighted to worship, there. And the look of
sadness in his dark eyes became a settled aspect.
Yet, here, there was much to interest and to excite
him. And he grew to look forward with pleasure to
his daily lessons.

At the end of three months, he was shipped to
France. There his seemingly aimless studies at the
training camp were put to active use.

At the foot of the long Flanders hill-slope the
"Here-We-Come" Regiment, of mixed American
and French infantry, held a caterpillar-shaped line
of trenches.

To the right, a few hundred yards away, was posted
a Lancashire regiment, supported by a battalion

from Cornwall. On the left were two French regiments. In front, facing the hill-slope and not a half-mile distant, was the geometric arrangement of sandbags that marked the contour of the German first-line trenches.

The hill behind them, the boches in front of them, French and British troops on either side of them-- the Here-We-Comes were helping to defend what was known as a "quiet' sector. Behind the hill, and on loftier heights far to the rear, the Allied artillery was posted. Somewhere in the same general locality lay a division of British reserves.

It is almost a waste of words to have described thus the surroundings of the Here-We-Comes. For, with no warning at all, those entire surroundings were about to be changed.

Ludendorff and his little playmates were just then engaged in the congenial sport of delivering unexpected blows at various successive points of the Allied line, in an effort to find some spot that was soft enough to cave in under the impact and let through a horde of gray-clad Huns. And though none of the defenders knew it, this "quiet" sector had been chosen for such a minor blow.

The men in higher command, back there behind the hill crest, had a belated inkling, though, of a proposed attack on the lightly defended front trenches. For the Allied airplanes which drifted in the upper heavens like a scattered handful of dragon-flies were not drifting there aimlessly. They were the eyes of the snakelike columns that crawled

so blindly on the scarred brown surface of the earth.
And those "eyes" had discerned the massing of a
force behind the German line had discerned and had
duly reported it.

The attack might come in a day. It might not come
in a week. But it was coming--unless the behind-
the-lines preparations were a gigantic feint.

A quiet dawn, in the quiet trenches of the quiet
sector. Desultory artillery and somewhat less
desultory sniping had prevailed throughout the
night, and at daybreak; but nothing out of the
ordinary.

Two men on listening-post had been shot; and so
had an overcurious sentry who peeped just an inch
too far above a parapet. A shell had burst in a
trench, knocking the telephone connection out of
gear and half burying a squad of sleepers under a lot
of earth. Otherwise, things were drowsily dull.

In a dugout sprawled Top-Sergeant Mahan,--
formerly of Uncle Sam's regular army, playing an
uninspiring game of poker with Sergeant Dale of
his company and Sergeant Vivier of the French
infantry. The Frenchman was slow in learning
poker's mysteries.

And, anyway, all three men were temporarily
penniless and were forced to play for I.O.U's--
which is stupid sport, at best.

So when, from the German line, came a quick sputt-
sputt-sputt from a half-dozen sharpshooters' rifles,

all three men looked up from their desultory game
in real interest. Mahan got to his feet with a grunt.

"Some other fool has been trying to see how far he
can rubber above the sandbags without drawing
boche fire," he hazarded, starting out to investigate.
"It's a miracle to me how a boche bullet can go
through heads that are so full of first-quality ivory
as those rubberers'."

But Mahan's strictures were quite unwarranted. The
sharpshooters were not firing at the parapet. Their
scattering shots were flying high, and hitting against
the slope of the hill behind the trenches.

Adown this shell--pocked hillside, as Mahan and
the other disturbed idlers gazed, came cantering a
huge dark-brown-and- white collie. The morning
wind stirred the black stippling that edged his tawny
fur, showing the gold-gray undercoat beneath it. His
white chest was like a snowdrift, and offered a fine
mark for the German rifles. A bullet or two sang
whiningly past his gayly up-flung head.

A hundred voices from the Here-We-Come trenches
hailed the advancing dog.

"Why, it's Bruce!" cried Mahan in glad welcome. "I
might 'a' known he or another of the collies would
be along. I might 'a' known it, when the telephones
went out of commission. He--"

"Regardez-donc!" interrupted the admiring Vivier.
"He acts like bullets was made of flies! Mooch he
care for boche lead-pills, ce brave vieux!"

"Yes," growled Dale worriedly; "and one of these days a bullet will find its way into that splendid carcass of his. He's been shot at, a thousand times, to my own knowledge. And all I ask is a chance, with a rifle-butt, at the skull of the Hun who downs him!"

"Downs Bruce?" queried Vivier in fine scorn. "The boche he is no borned who can do it. Bruce has what you call it, in Ainglish, the 'charm life.' He go safe, where other caniche be pepper- potted full of holes. I've watch heem. I know."

Unscathed by the several shots that whined past him, Bruce came to a halt at the edge of a traverse. There he stood, wagging his plume of a tail in grave friendliness, while a score of khaki- clad arms reached up to lift him bodily into the trench.

A sergeant unfastened the message from the dog's collar and posted off to the colonel with it.

The message was similar to one which had been telephoned to each of the supporting bodies, to right and to left of the Here-We- Comes. It bade the colonel prepare to withdraw his command from the front trenches at nightfall, and to move back on the main force behind the hill-crest. The front trenches were not important; and they were far too lightly manned to resist a mass attack. Wherefore the drawing-in and consolidating of the whole outflung line.

Bruce, his work done now, had leisure to respond to the countless offers of hospitality that encompassed him. One man brought him a slice of cold broiled bacon. Another spread pork-grease over a bit of bread and proffered it. A third unearthed from some sacredly guarded hiding-place an excessively stale half-inch square of sweet chocolate.

Had the dog so chosen, he might then and there have eaten himself to death on the multitude of votive offerings. But in a few minutes he had had enough, and he merely sniffed in polite refusal at all further gifts.

"See?" lectured Mahan. "That's the beast of it! When you say a fellow eats or drinks 'like a beast,' you ought to remember that a beast won't eat or drink a mouthful more than is good for him."

"Gee!" commented the somewhat corpulent Dale. "I'm glad I'm not a beast--especially on pay-day."

Presently Bruce tired of the ovation tendered him. These ovations were getting to be an old story. They had begun as far back as his training-camp days--when the story of his joining the army was told by the man to whom The Place's guest had written commending the dog to the trainers' kindness.

At the training-camp this story had been reenforced by the chief collie-teacher--a dour little Hieland Scot named McQuibigaskie, who on the first day declared that the American dog had more sense and more promise and more soul "than a' t'other tykes south o' Kirkcudbright Brae."

Being only mortal, Bruce found it pleasanter to be
admired and petted than ignored or kicked. He was
impersonally friendly with the soldiers, when he
was off duty; and he relished the dainties they were
forever thrusting at him.

But at times his soft eyes would grow dark with
homesickness for the quiet loveliness of The Place
and for the Mistress and the Master who were his
loyally worshiped gods. Life had been so happy and
so sweetly uneventful for him, at The Place! And
there had been none of the awful endless thunder
and the bewilderingly horrible smells and gruesome
sights which here met him at every turn.

The dog's loving heart used to grow sick with it all;
and he longed unspeakably for home. But he was a
gallant soldier, and he did his work not only well,
but with a snap and a dash and an almost uncanny
intelligence which made him an idol to the men.

Presently, now, having eaten all he wanted and
having been patted and talked to until he craved
solitude, Bruce strolled ever to an empty dugout,
curled up on a torn blanket there, put his nose
between his white paws and went to sleep.

The German artillery-fire had swelled from an
occasional explosion to a ceaseless roar, that made
the ground vibrate and heave, and that beat on the
eardrums with nauseating iterance. But it did not
bother Bruce. For months he had been used to this
sort of annoyance, and he had learned to sleep
snugly through it all.

Meanwhile, outside his dugout, life was speeding up at a dizzying rate. The German artillery had sprung to sudden and wholesale activity. Far to the right of the Here-We-Come regiment's trenches a haze had begun to crawl along the ground and to send snaky tendrils high in air-tendrils that blended into a single grayish-green wall as they moved forward. The hazewall's gray- green was shot by yellow and purple tinges as the sun's weak rays touched it. To the left of the Here-We-Comes, and then in front of them, appeared the same wall of billowing gas.

The Here-We-Comes were ready for it with their hastily donned masks. But there was no need of the precaution. By one of the sudden wind--freaks so common in the story of the war, the gas- cloud was cleft in two by a swirling breeze, and it rolled dankly on, to right and left, leaving the central trenches clear.

Now, an artillery barrage, accompanied or followed by a gas- demonstration, can mean but one thing: a general attack. Therefore telephonic word came to the detachments to left and right of the Here-We-Comes, to fall back, under cover of the gas- cloud, to safer positions. Two dogs were sent, with the same order, to the Here-We-Comes. (One of the dogs was gassed. A bit of shrapnel found the other.)

Thus it was that the Here-We-Comes were left alone (though they did not know it), to hold the position,--with no support on either side, and with a mere handful of men wherewith to stem the impending rush.

On the heels of the dispersing gas-cloud, and straight across the half-mile or less of broken ground, came a line of gray. In five successive waves, according to custom, the boches charged. Each wave hurled itself forward as fast as efficiency would let it, in face of the opposing fire, and as far as human endurance would be goaded. Then it went down, and its survivors attached themselves to the succeeding wave.

Hence, by the time the fifth and mightiest wave got into motion, it was swelled by the survivors of all four of its predecessors and was an all-but-resistless mass of shouting and running men.

The rifles and machine-guns of the Here-We-Comes played merrily into the advancing gray swarms, stopping wave after wave, and at last checking the fifth and "master" wave almost at the very brink of the Franco-American parapet.

"That's how they do!" Mahan pantingly explained to a rather shaky newcomer, as the last wave fell back. "They count on numbers and bullrushes to get them there. If they'd had ten thousand men, in that rush, instead of five thousand, they'd have got us. And if they had twice as many men in their whole army as they have, they'd win this war. But praise be, they haven't twice as many! That is one of the fifty-seven reasons why the Allies are going to lick Germany."

Mahan talked jubilantly. The same jubilation ran all along the line of victors. But the colonel and his staff were not rejoicing. They had just learned of the withdrawal of the forces to either side of them, and they knew they themselves could not hope to stand against a second and larger charge.

Such a charge the enemy were certain to make. The Germans, too, must soon learn of the defection of the supports. It was now only a question of an hour or less before a charge with a double- enveloping movement would surround and bag the Here-We-Comes, catching the whole regiment in an inescapable trap.

To fall back, now, up that long bare hillside, under full fire of the augmented German artillery, would mean a decimating of the entire command. The Here-We-Comes could not retreat. They could not hope to hold their ground. The sole chance for life lay in the arrival of strong reenforcements from the rear, to help them hold the trenches until night, or to man the supporting positions. Reserves were within easy striking distance. But, as happened so many times in the war, there was no routine way to summon them in time.

It was the chance sight of a crumpled message lying on his dugout-table that reminded the colonel of Bruce's existence and of his presence in the front trench. It was a matter of thirty seconds for the colonel to scrawl an urgent appeal and a brief statement of conditions. Almost as soon as the note was ready, an orderly appeared at the dugout entrance, convoying the newly awakened Bruce.

The all-important message was fastened in place. The colonel himself went to the edge of the traverse, and with his own arms lifted the eighty-pound collie to the top.

There was tenderness as well as strength in the lifting arms. As he set Bruce down on the brink, the colonel said, as if speaking to a fellow-human:

"I hate to do it, old chap. I HATE to! There isn't one chance in three of your getting all the way up the hill alive. But there wouldn't be one chance in a hundred, for a MAN. The boches will be on the lookout for just this move. And their best sharpshooters will be waiting for you--even if you dodge the shrapnel and the rest of the artillery. I'm sorry! And--good-by."

Then, tersely, he rasped out the command--

"Bruce! Headquarters! Headquarters! QUICK!"

At a bound, the dog was gone.

Breasting the rise of the hill, Bruce set off at a sweeping run, his tawny-and-white mane flying in the wind.

A thousand eyes, from the Here-We-Come trenches, watched his flight. And as many eyes from the German lines saw the huge collie's dash up the coverless slope.

Scarce had Bruce gotten fairly into his stride when the boche bullets began to sing--not a desultory little flurry of shots, as before; but by the score, and with a murderous earnestness. When he had appeared, on his way to the trenches, an hour earlier, the Germans had opened fire on him, merely for their own amusement-- upon the same merry principle which always led them to shoot at an Ally war-dog. But now they understood his all-important mission; and they strove with their best skill to thwart it.

The colonel of the Here-We-Comes drew his breath sharply between his teeth. He did not regret the sending of the collie. It had been a move of stark military necessity. And there was an off chance that it might mean the saving of his whole command.

But the colonel was fond of Bruce, and it angered him to hear the frantic effort of the boche marksmen to down so magnificent a creature. The bullets were spraying all about the galloping dog, kicking up tiny swirls of dust at his heels and in front of him and to either side.

Mahan, watching, with streaming eyes and blaspheming lips, recalled the French sergeant's theory that Bruce bore a charmed life. And he prayed that Vivier might be right. But in his prayer was very little faith. For under such a fusillade it seemed impossible that at least one highpower bullet should not reach the collie before the slope could be traversed. A fast-running dog is not an easy mark for a bullet--especially if the dog be a collie, with a trace of wolf--ancestry in his gait. A dog, at best, does not gallop straight ahead as does a horse. There is almost always a sidewise lilt to his run.

Bruce was still further aided by the shell-plowed
condition of the hillside. Again and again he had to
break his stride, to leap some shell-hole. Often he
had to encircle such holes. More than once he
bounded headlong down into a gaping crater and
scrambled up its far side. These erratic moves, and
the nine-hundred-yard distance (a distance that was
widening at every second) made the sharpshooters'
task anything but an exact science.

Mahan's gaze followed the dog's every step. Bruce
had cleared more than three-fourths of the slope.
The top-sergeant permitted himself the luxury of a
broad grin.

"I'll buy Vivier all the red-ink wine he can gargle,
next pay- day!" he vowed. "He was dead right about
the dog. No bullet was ever molded that can get--"

Mahan broke off in his exultation, with an
explosive oath, as a new note in the firing smote
upon his trained hearing.

"The swine!" he roared. "The filthy, unsportsmanly,
dog-eating Prussian swine! They're turning
MACHINE-GUNS on him!"

In place of the intermittent rattle of rifleshots now
came the purring cough of rapidfire guns. The
bullets hit the upper hillside in swathes, beginning a
few yards behind the flying collie and moving
upward toward him like a sweeping of an unseen
scythe.

"That's the wind-up!" groaned Mahan. "Lord, send

me an even break against one of those Hun
machinegunners some day! If--"

Again Mahan failed to finish his train of thought.
He stared open-mouthed up the hill. Almost at the
very summit, within a rod or two of the point where
the crest would intervene between him and his foes,
Bruce whirled in mid-air and fell prone.

The fast-following swaths of machine-gun bullets
had not reached him. But another German enemy
had. From behind a heap of offal, on the crest, a
yellow-gray dog had sprung, and had launched
himself bodily upon Bruce's flank as the unnoticing
collie had flashed past him.

The assailant was an enormous and hyena-like
German police-dog. He was one of the many of his
breed that were employed (for work or food) in the
German camps, and which used to sneak away from
their hard-kicking soldier-owners to ply a more
congenial trade as scavengers, and as seekers for
the dead. For, in traits as well as in looks, the
police-dog often emulates the ghoulish hyena.

Seeing the approaching collie (always inveterate foe
of his kind), the police-dog had gauged the distance
and had launched his surprise attack with true
Teuton sportsmanship and efficiency. Down went
Bruce under the fierce weight that crashed against
his shoulder. But before the other could gain his
coveted throat-grip, Bruce was up again. Like a
furry whirlwind he was at the police-dog, fighting
more like a wolf than a civilized collie --tearing into
his opponent with a maniac rage, snapping,

slashing; his glittering white fangs driving at a
dozen vulnerable points in a single second.

It was as though Bruce knew he had no time to
waste from his life-and-death mission. He could not
elude this enemy, so he must finish him as quickly
as possible.

"Give me your rifle!" sputtered Mahan to the soldier
nearest him. "I'll take one potshot at that Prussian
cur, before the machine- guns get the two of 'em.
Even if I hit Bruce by mistake, he'd rather die by a
Christian Yankee-made bullet than--"

Just then the scythelike machine-gun fire reached
the hillcrest combatants. And in the same instant a
shell smote the ground, apparently between them.
Up went a geyser of smoke and dirt and rocks.
When the cloud settled, there was a deep gully in
the ground where a moment earlier Bruce and the
police-dog had waged their death-battle.

"That settles it!" muttered the colonel.

And he went to make ready for such puny defense
as his men might hope to put up against the German
rush.

While these futile preparations were still under way,
terrific artillery fire burst from the Allied batteries
behind the hill, shielding the Here-We-Come
trenches with a curtain of fire whose lower folds
draped themselves right unlovingly around the
German lines. Under cover of this barrage, down
the hill swarmed the Allied reserves!

"How did you get word?" demanded the astonished colonel of the Here-We-Comes, later in the day.

"From your note, of course," replied the general he had questioned. "The collie--old Bruce."

"Bruce?" babbled the colonel foolishly.

"Of course," answered the general. "Who else? But I'm afraid it's the last message he'll ever deliver. He came rolling and staggering up to headquarters--one mass of blood, and three inches thick with caked dirt. His right side was torn open from a shell-wound, and he had two machine-gun bullets in his shoulder. He's deaf as a post, too, from shell-shock. He tumbled over in a heap on the steps of headquarters. But he GOT there. That's Bruce, all over. That's the best type of collie, all over. Some of us were for putting him out of his misery with a shot through the head. We'd have done it, too, if it had been any other dog. But the surgeon-general waded in and took a hand in the game-- carried Bruce to his own quarters. We left him working over the dog himself. And he swears Bruce will pull through!"

CHAPTER IV.

When Eyes Were No Use

"Yes, it's an easy enough trade to pick up," lectured Top- Sergeant Mahan, formerly of the regular army.

"You've just got to remember a few things. But you've got to keep on remembering those few, all the time. If you forget one of 'em, it's the last bit of forgetting you're ever likely to do."

Top-Sergeant Mahan, of the mixed French-and-American regiment known as "Here-We-Come," was squatting at ease on the trench firing-- step. From that professorial seat he was dispensing useful knowledge to a group of fellow-countrymen-newly arrived from the base, to pad the "Here-We-Come" ranks, which had been thinned at the Rache attack.

"What sort of things have we got to remember, Sergeant?" jauntily asked a lanky Missourian. " We've got the drill pretty pat; and the trench instructions and--"

"Gee!" ejaculated Mahan. "I had no idea of that! Then why don't you walk straight ahead into Berlin? If you know all you say you do, about war, there's nothing more for you to learn. I'll drop a line to General Foch and suggest to him that you rookies be detailed to teach the game to us oldsters."

"I didn't mean to be fresh," apologized the jaunty one. "Won't you go ahead and tell us the things we need to remember?"

"Well," exhorted Mahan, appeased by the newcomer's humility, "there aren't so many of them, after all. Learn to duck, when you hear a Minnie grunt or a whizzbang cut loose; or a five-nine begin to whimper. Learn not to bother to duck when the rifles get to jabbering--for you'll never hear the bullet that gets you. Study the nocturnal habits of machine-guns and the ways of snipers and the right time not to play the fool. And keep saying to yourself: 'The bullet ain't molded that can get ME!' Mean it when you say it. When you've learned those few things, the rest of the war-game is dead easy."

"Except," timidly amended old Sergeant Vivier, the gray little Frenchman, "except when eyes are--are what you call it, no use." "That's right," assented Mahan. "In the times when eyes are no use, all rules fail. And then the only thing you can do is to trust to your Yankee luck. I remember--"

"'When eyes are no use'?" repeated the recruit. "If you mean after dark, at night--haven't we got the searchlights and the starshells and all that?"

"Son," replied Mahan, "we have. Though I don't see how you ever guessed such an important secret. But since you know everything, maybe you'll just kindly tell us what good all the lights in the world are going to do us when the filthy yellow-gray fog begins to ooze up out of the mud and the shell-holes, and the filthy gray mist oozes down from the clouds to meet it. Fog is the one thing that all the war--science won't overcome. A fogpenetrator hasn't been invented yet. If it had been, there'd be many a husky lad living today, who has gone West, this past few years, on account of the fogs. Fog is the boche's pet. It gives Fritzy a lovely chance to creep up or, us. It--"

"It is the helper of US, too," suggested old Vivier. "More than one time, it has kept me safe when I was on patrol. And did it not help to save us at Rache, when--"

"The fog may have helped us, one per cent, at Rache," admitted Mahan. "But Bruce did ninety-nine per cent of the saving."

"A Scotch general?" asked the recruit, as Vivier nodded cordial affirmation of Mahan's words, and as others of the old-timers muttered approval.

"No," contradicted Mahan. "A Scotch collie. If you were dry behind the ears, in this life, you wouldn't have to ask who Bruce is."

"I don't understand," faltered the rookie, suspicious of a possible joke.

"You will soon," Mahan told him. "Bruce will be here to-day. I heard the K.O. saying the big dog is going to be sent down with some dispatches or something, from headquarters. It's his first trip since he was cut up so."

"I am saving him--this!" proclaimed Vivier, disgorging from the flotsam of his pocket a lump of once-white sugar. "My wife, she smuggle three of these to me in her last paquet. One I eat in my cafe noir; one I present to mon cher vieux, ce bon Mahan; one I keep for the grand dog what save us all that day."

"What's the idea?" queried the mystified rookie. "I don't--"

"We were stuck in the front line of the Rache salient," explained Mahan, eager to recount his dog-friend's prowess. "On both sides our supports got word to fall back. We couldn't get the word, because our telephone connection was knocked galley-west. There we were, waiting for a Hun attack to wipe us out. We couldn't fall back, for they were peppering the hillslope behind us. We were at the bottom. They'd have cut us to ribbons if we'd shown our carcasses in the open. Bruce was here, with a message he'd brought. The K.O. sent him back to headquarters for the reserves. The boche heavies and snipers and machine-guns all cut loose to stop him as he scooted up the hill. And a measly giant of a German police dog tried to kill him, too. Bruce got through the lot of them; and he reached headquarters with the SOS call that saved us. The poor chap was cut and gouged and torn by bullets and shell-scraps, and he was nearly dead from shell-shock, too. But the surgeon general worked over him, himself, and pulled him back to life. He--"

"He is a loved pet of a man and a woman in your America, I have heard one say," chimed in Vivier. "And his home, there, was in the quiet country. He was lent to the cause, as a patriotic offering, ce brave! And of a certainty, he has earned his welcome."

When Bruce, an hour later, trotted into the trenches, on the way to the "Here-We-Come" colonel's quarters, he was received like a visiting potentate. Dozens of men hailed him eagerly by name as he made his way to his destination with the message affixed to his collar.

Many of these men were his well-remembered
friends and comrades. Mahan and Vivier, and one
or two more, he had grown to like--as well as he
could like any one in that land of horrors, three
thousand miles away from The Place, where he was
born, and from the Mistress and the Master, who
were his loyally worshiped gods.

Moreover, being only mortal and afflicted with a
hearty appetite, Bruce loved the food and other
delicacies the men were forever offering him as a
variation on the stodgy fare dished out to him and
his fellow war-dogs.

As much to amuse and interest the soldiers whose
hero he was, as for any special importance in the
dispatch he carried, Bruce had been sent now to the
trenches of the Here-We-Comes. It was his first
visit to the regiment he had saved, since the days of
the Rache assault two months earlier. Thanks to
supremely clever surgery and to tender care, the dog
was little the worse for his wounds. His hearing
gradually had come back. In one shoulder he had a
very slight stiffness which was not a limp, and a
new-healed furrow scarred the left side of his tawny
coat. Otherwise he was as good as new.

As Bruce trotted toward the group that so recently
had been talking of him, the Missouri recruit
watched with interest for the dog's joy at this
reunion with his old friends. Bruce's snowy chest
and black-stippled coat were fluffed out by many
recent baths. His splendid head high and his dark
eyes bright, the collie advanced toward the group.

Mahan greeted him joyously. Vivier stretched out a
hand which displayed temptingly the long-hoarded
lump of sugar. A third man produced, from nowhere
in particular, a large and meat-fringed soup-bone.

"I wonder which of you he'll come to, first," said the
interested Missourian.

The question was answered at once, and right
humiliatingly. For Bruce did not falter in his
swinging stride as he came abreast of the group.
Not by so much as a second glance did he notice
Mahan's hail and the tempting food.

As he passed within six inches of the lump of sugar
which Vivier was holding out to him, the dog's
silken ears quivered slightly, sure sign of hard-
repressed emotion in a thoroughbred collie,-- but he
gave no other manifestation that he knew any one
was there.

"Well, I'll be blessed!" snickered the Missourian in
high derision, as Bruce passed out of sight around
an angle of the trench. "So that's the pup who is
such a pal of you fellows, is he? Gee, but it was a
treat to see how tickled he was to meet you again!"

To the rookie's amazement none of his hearers
seemed in the least chagrined over the dogs chilling
disregard of them. Instead, Mahan actually grunted
approbation.

"He'll be back," prophesied the Sergeant. "Don't
you worry. He'll be back. We ought to have had
more sense than try to stop him when he's on duty.

He has better discipline than the rest of us. That's one of very first things they teach a courier-dog--to pay no attention to anybody, when he's on dispatch duty. When Bruce has delivered his message to the K.O., he'll have the right to hunt up his chums. And no one knows it better'n Bruce himself."

"It was a sin--a thoughtlessness--of me to hold the sugar at him," said old Vivier. "Ah, but he is a so good soldier, ce brave Bruce! He look not to the left nor yet to the right, nor yet to the so-desired sugar-lump. He keep his head at attention! All but the furry tips of his ears. Them he has not yet taught to be good soldiers. They tremble, when he smell the sugar and the good soup-bone. They quiver like the little leaf. But he keep on. He- -"

There was a scurry of fast-cantering feet. Around the angle of the trench dashed Bruce. Head erect, soft dark eyes shining with a light of gay mischief, he galloped up to the grinning Sergeant Vivier and stood. The dog's great plume of a tail was wagging violently. His tulip ears were cocked. His whole interest in life was fixed on the precious lump of sugar which Vivier held out to him.

From puppyhood, Bruce had adored lump sugar. Even at The Place, sugar had been a rarity for him, for the Mistress and the Master had known the damage it can wreak upon a dog's teeth and digestion. Yet, once in a while, as a special luxury, the Mistress had been wont to give him a solitary lump of sugar.

Since his arrival in France, the dog had never seen

nor scented such a thing until now. Yet he did not
jump for the gift. He did not try to snatch it from
Vivier. Instead, he waited until the old Frenchman
held it closer toward him, with the invitation:

"Take it, mon vieux! It is for you."

Then and then only did Bruce reach daintily
forward and grip the grimy bit of sugar between his
mighty jaws. Vivier stroked the collie's head while
Bruce wagged his tail and munched the sugar and
blinked gratefully up at the donor. Mahan looked
on, enviously. "A dog's got forty-two teeth, instead
of the thirty- two that us humans have to chew on,"
observed the Sergeant. "A vet' told me that once.
And sugar is bad for all forty-two of 'em. Maybe
you didn't know that, Monsoo Vivier? Likely, at
this rate, we'll have to chip in before long and buy
poor Brucie a double set of false teeth. Just because
you've put his real ones out of business with lumps
of sugar!"

Vivier looked genuinely concerned at this grim
forecast. Bruce wandered across to the place where
the donor of the soup-bone brandished his offering.
Other men, too, were crowding around with gifts.

Between petting and feeding, the collie spent a busy
hour among his comrades-at-arms. He was to stay
with the "Here-We-Comes" until the following day,
and then carry back to headquarters a
reconnaissance report.

At four o'clock that afternoon the sky was softly
blue and the air was unwontedly clear. By five

o'clock a gentle India-summer haze blurred the world's sharper outlines. By six a blanket-fog rolled in, and the air was wetly unbreatheable. The fog lay so thick over the soggy earth that objects ten feet away were invisible.

"This," commented Sergeant Mahan, "is one of the times I was talking about this morning--when eyes are no use. This is sure the country for fogs, in war-time. The cockneys tell me the London fogs aren't a patch on 'em."

The "Here-We-Comes" were encamped, for the while, at the edge of a sector from whence all military importance had recently been removed by a convulsive twist of a hundred-mile battle-front. In this dull hole-in-a-corner the new-arrived rivets were in process of welding into the more veteran structure of the mixed regiment.

Not a quarter-mile away--across No Man's Land and athwart two barriers of barbed wire--lay a series of German trenches. Now, in all probability, and from all outward signs, the occupants of this boche position consisted only of a regiment or two which had been so badly cut up, in a foiled drive, as to need a month of non-exciting routine before going back into more perilous service.

Yet the commander of the division to which the "Here-We-Comes" were attached did not trust to probabilities nor to outward signs. He had been at the front long enough to realize that the only thing likely to happen was the thing which seemed unlikeliest. And he felt a morbid curiosity to learn more about the personnel of those dormant German trenches.

Wherefore he had sent an order that a handful of the "Here-We- Comes" go forth into No Man's Land, on the first favorable night, and try to pick up a boche prisoner or two for questioning- purposes. A scouring of the doubly wired area between the hostile lines might readily harvest some solitary sentinel or some other man on special duty, or even the occupants of a listening-post. And the division commander earnestly desired to question such prisoner or prisoners. The fog furnished an ideal night for such an expedition.

Thus it was that a very young lieutenant and Sergeant Mahan and ten privates--the lanky Missourian among them--were detailed for the prisoner-seeking job. At eleven o'clock, they crept over the top, single file.

It was a night wherein a hundred searchlights and a million star- -flares would not have made more impression on the density of the fog than would the striking of a safety match. Yet the twelve reconnoiterers were instructed to proceed in the cautious manner customary to such nocturnal expeditions into No Man's Land. They moved forward at the lieutenant's order, tiptoeing abreast, some twenty feet apart from one another, and advancing in three-foot strides. At every thirty steps the entire line was required to halt and to reestablish contact--in other words, to "dress" on the l ieutenant, who was at the extreme right.

This maneuver was more time-wasting and less simple than its recital would imply. For in the dark, unaccustomed legs are liable to miscalculation in the matter of length of stride, even when shell-holes and other inequalities of ground do not complicate the calculations still further. And it is hard to maintain a perfectly straight line when moving forward through choking fog and over scores of obstacles.

The halts for realignment consumed much time and caused no little confusion. Nervousness began to encompass the Missouri recruit. He was as brave as the next man. But there is something creepy about walking with measured tread through an invisible space, with no sound but the stealthy pad-pad-pad of equally hesitant footsteps twenty feet away on either side. The Missourian was grateful for the intervals that brought the men into mutual contact, as the eerie march continued.

The first line of barbed wire was cut and passed. Then followed an endless groping progress across No Man's Land, and several delays, as one man or another had trouble in finding contact with his neighbor.

At last the party came to the German wires. The lieutenant had drawn on a rubber glove. In his gloved hand he grasped a strip of steel which he held in front of him, like a wand, fanning the air with it.

As he came to the entanglement, he probed the barbed wire carefully with his wand, watching for

an ensuing spark. For the Germans more than once
had been known to electrify their wires, with fatal
results to luckless prowlers.

These wires, to-night, were not charged. And, with
pliers, the lieutenant and Mahan started to cut a
passageway through them.

As the very first strand parted under his pressure,
Mahan laid one hand warningly on the lieutenant's
sleeve, and then passed the same prearranged
warning down the line to the left.

Silence--moveless, tense, sharply listening silence--
followed his motion. Then the rest of the party
heard the sound which Mahan's keener ears had
caught a moment earlier--the thud of many
marching feet. Here was no furtive creeping, as
when the twelve Yankees had moved along. Rather
was it the rhythmic beat of at least a hundred pairs
of shapeless army boots--perhaps of more. The
unseen marchers were moving wordlessly, but with
no effort at muffling the even tread of their multiple
feet.

"They're coming this way!" breathed Sergeant
Mahan almost without sound, his lips close to the
excited young lieutenant's ear. "And they're not fifty
paces off. That means they're boches. So near the
German wire, our men would either be crawling or
else charging, not marching! It's a company--maybe
a battalion--coming back from a reconnaissance,
and making for a gap in their own wire some where
near here. If we lay low there's an off chance they
may pass us by."

Without awaiting the lieutenant's order, Mahan passed along the signal for every man to drop to earth and lie there. He all but forced the eagerly gesticulating lieutenant to the ground.

On came the swinging tread of the Germans. Mahan, listening breathlessly, tried to gauge the distance and the direction. He figured, presently, that the break the Germans had made in their wire could be only a few yards below the spot where he and the lieutenant had been at work with the pliers. Thus the intruders, from their present course, must inevitably pass very close to the prostrate Americans--so close, perhaps, as to brush against the nearest of them, or even to step on one or more of the crouching figures.

Mahan whispered to the man on his immediate left, the rookie from Missouri:

"Edge closer to the wire--close as you can wiggle, and lie flat. Pass on the word."

The Missourian obeyed. Before writhing his long body forward against the bristly mass of wire he passed the instructions on to the man at his own left.

But his nerves were at breaking-point.

It had been bad enough to crawl through the blind fog, with the ghostly steps of his comrades pattering softly at either side of him. But it was a thousand times harder to lie helpless here, in the choking fog and on the soaked ground, while countless enemies were bearing down, unseen, upon him, on one side, and an impenetrable wire cut off his retreat on the other.

The Missourian had let his imagination begin to work; always a mistake in a private soldier. He was visualizing the moment when this tramping German force should become aware of the presence of their puny foes and should slaughter them against the merciless wires. It would not be a fair stand-up fight, this murder-rush of hundreds of men against twelve who were penned in and could not maneuver nor escape. And the thought of it was doing queer things to the rookie's overwrought nerves.

Having passed the word to creep closer to the wires, he began to execute the order in person, with no delay at all. But he was a fraction of a second too late. The Germans were moving in hike- formation with "points" thrown out in advance to either side-- a "point" being a private soldier who, for scouting and other purposes, marches at some distance from the main body.

The point, ahead of the platoon, had swerved too far to the left, in the blackness--an error that would infallibly have brought him up against the wires, with considerable force, in another two steps. But the Missourian was between him and the wires. And the point's heavy-shod foot came down, heel first, on the back of the rookie's out-groping hand. Such a crushing impact, on the hand-back, is one of the most agonizing minor injuries a man can sustain. And this fact the Missourian discovered with great suddenness.

His too-taut nerves forced from his throat a yell that split the deathly stillness with an ear-piercing vehemence. He sprang to his feet, forgetful of orders intent only on thrusting his bayonet through the Hun who had caused such acute torture to his hand. Half way up, the rookie's feet went out from under him in the slimy mud. He caromed against the point, then fell headlong.

The German, doubtless thinking he had stumbled upon a single stray American scout, whirled his own rifle aloft, to dash out the brains of his luckless foe. But before the upflung butt could descend,-- before the rookie could rise or dodge,--the point added his quota to the rude breaking of the night's silence. He screamed in panic terror, dropped his brandished gun and reeled backward, clawing at his own throat.

For out of the eerie darkness, something had launched itself at him--something silent and terrible, that had flown to the Missourian's aid. Down with a crash went the German, on his back. He rolled against the Missourian, who promptly sought to grapple with him.

But even as he clawed for the German, the rookie's nerves wrung from him a second yell--this time less of rage than of horror.

"Sufferin' cats!" he bellowed. "Why didn't anybody ever tell me Germans was covered with fur instead of clothes?"

The boche platoon was no longer striding along in

hike- formation. It was broken up into masses of wildly running men, all of them bearing down upon the place whence issued this ungodly racket and turmoil. Stumbling, reeling, blindly falling and rising again, they came on.

Some one among them loosed a rifle-shot in the general direction of the yelling. A second and a third German rifleman followed the example of the first. From the distant American trenches, one or two snipers began to pepper away toward the enemy lines, though the fog was too thick for them, to see the German rifle-flashes.

The boches farthest to the left, in the blind rush, fouled with the wires. German snipers, from behind the Hun parapets, opened fire. A minute earlier the night had been still as the grave. Now it fairly vibrated with clangor. All because one rookie's nerves had been less staunch than his courage, and because that same rookie had not only had his hand stepped on in the dark, but had encountered something swirling and hairy when he grabbed for the soldier who had stepped on him!

The American lieutenant, at the onset of the clamor, sprang to his feet, whipping out his pistol; his dry lips parted in a command to charge--a command which, naturally, would have reduced his eleven men and himself to twelve corpses or to an equal number of mishandled prisoners within the next few seconds. But a big hand was clapped unceremoniously across the young officer's mouth, silencing the half-spoken suicidal order.

Sergeant Mahan's career in the regular army had given him an almost uncanny power of sizing up his fellowmen. And he had long ago decided that this was the sort of thing his untried lieutenant would be likely to do, in just such an emergency. Wherefore his flagrant breach of discipline in shoving his palm across the mouth of his superior officer.

And as he was committing this breach of discipline, he heard the Missourian's strangled gasp of:

"Why didn't anybody ever tell me Germans was covered with fur?"

In a flash Mahan understood. Wheeling, he stooped low and flung out both arms in a wide-sweeping circle. Luckily his right hand's fingertips, as they completed the circle, touched something fast-moving and furry.

"Bruce!" he whispered fiercely, tightening his precarious grip on the wisp of fur his fingers had touched. "Bruce! Stand still, boy! It's YOU who's got to get us clear of this! Nobody else, short of the good Lord, can do it!"

Bruce had had a pleasantly lazy day with his friends in the first-line trenches. There had been much good food and more petting. And at last, comfortably tired of it all, he had gone to sleep. He had awakened in a most friendly mood, and a little hungry. Wherefore he had sallied forth in search of human companionship. He found plenty of soldiers who were more than willing to talk to him and make much of him. But, a little farther ahead, he saw his

good friend, Sergeant Mahan, and others of his
acquaintances, starting over the parapet on what
promised to be a jolly evening stroll.

All dogs find it hard to resist the mysterious lure of
a walk in human companionship. True, the night
was not an ideal one for a ramble, and the fog had a
way of congealing wetly on Bruce's shaggy coat.
Still, a damp coat was not enough of a discomfort to
offset the joy of a stroll with his friends. So Bruce
had followed the twelve men quietly into No Man's
Land, falling decorously into step behind Mahan.

It had not been much of a walk, for speed or for fun.
For the humans went ridiculously slowly, and had
an eccentric way of bunching together, every now
and again, and then of stringing out into a
shambling line. Still, it was a walk, and therefore
better than loafing behind in the trenches. And
Bruce had kept his noiseless place at the Sergeant's
heels.

Then--long before Mahan heard the approaching
tramp of feet-- Bruce caught not only the sound but
the scent of the German platoon. The scent at once
told him that the strangers were not of his own
army. A German soldier and an American soldier--
because of their difference in diet as well as for
certain other and more cogent reasons--have by no
means the same odor, to a collie's trained scent, nor
to that of other breeds of war-dogs. Official records
of dog-sentinels prove that.

Aliens were nearing Bruce's friends. And the dog's
ruff began to stand up. But Mahan and the rest

seemed in no way concerned in spirit thereby--
though, to the dog's understanding, they must surely
be aware of the approach. So Bruce gave no further
sign of displeasure. He was out for a walk, as a
guest. He was not on sentry-duty.

But when the nearest German was almost upon
them, and all twelve Americans dropped to the
ground, the collie became interested once more. A
German stepped on the hand of one of his newest
friends. And the friend yelled in pain. Whereat the
German made as if to strike the stepped-on man.

This was quite enough for loyal Bruce. Without so
much as a growl of warning, he jumped at the
offender.

Dog and man tumbled earthward together. Then
after an instant of flurry and noise, Bruce felt
Mahan's fingers on his shoulder and heard the stark
appeal of Mahan's whispered voice. Instantly the
dog was a professional soldier once more--alertly
obedient and resourceful.

"Catch hold my left arm, Lieutenant!" Mahan was
exhorting. "Close up, there, boys--every man's hand
grabbing tight to the shoulder of the man on his left!
Pass the word. And you, Missouri, hang onto the
Lieutenant! Quick, there! And tread soft and tread
fast, and don't let go, whatever happens! Not a
sound out of any one! I'm leading the way. And
Bruce is going to lead me."

There was a scurrying scramble as the men groped
for one another. Mahan tightened his hold on

Bruce's mane.

"Bruce!" he said, very low, but with a strength of appeal that was not lost on the listening dog. "Bruce! Camp! Back to CAMP! And keep QUIET! Back to camp, boy! CAMP!"

He had no need to repeat his command so often and so strenuously. Bruce was a trained courier. The one word "Camp!" was quite enough to tell him what he was to do.

Turning, he faced the American lines and tried to break into a gallop. His scent and his knowledge of direction were all the guides he needed. A dog always relies on his nose first and his eyes last. The fog was no obstacle at all to the collie. He understood the Sergeant's order, and he set out at once to obey it.

But at the very first step, he was checked. Mahan did not release that feverishly tight hold on his mane, but merely shifted to his collar.

Bruce glanced back, impatient at the delay. But Mahan did not let go. Instead he said once more:

"CAMP, boy!"

And Bruce understood he was expected to make his way to camp, with Mahan hanging on to his collar.

Bruce did not enjoy this mode of locomotion. It was inconvenient, and there seemed no sense in it; but

there were many things about this strenuous war-
trade that Bruce neither enjoyed nor comprehended,
yet which he performed at command.

So again he turned campward, Mahan at his collar
and an annoyingly hindering tail of men stumbling
silently on behind them. All around were the
Germans--butting drunkenly through the blanket-
dense fog, swinging their rifles like flails, shouting
confused orders, occasionally firing. Now and then
two or more of them would collide and would
wrestle in blind fury, thinking they had encountered
an American.

Impeded by their own sightlessly swarming
numbers, as much as by the impenetrable darkness,
they sought the foe. And but for Bruce they must
quickly have found what they sought. Even in
compact form, the Americans could not have had
the sheer luck to dodge every scattered contingent
of Huns which starred the German end of No Man's
Land--most of them between the fugitives and the
American lines.

But Bruce was on dispatch duty. It was his work to
obey commands and to get back to camp at once. It
was bad enough to be handicapped by Mahan's
grasp on his collar. He was not minded to suffer
further delay by running into any of the clumps of
gesticulating and cabbage-reeking Germans
between him and his goal. So he steered clear of
such groups, making several wide detours in order
to do so. Once or twice he stopped short to let some
of the Germans grope past him, not six feet away.
Again he veered sharply to the left--increasing his

pace and forcing Mahan and the rest to increase theirs--to avoid a squad of thirty men who were quartering the field in close formation, and who all but jostled the dog as they strode sightlessly by. An occasional rifle-shot spat forth its challenge. From both trench-lines men were firing at a venture. A few of the bullets sang nastily close to the twelve huddled men and their canine leader. Once a German, not three yards away, screamed aloud and fell sprawling and kicking, as one such chance bullet found him. Above and behind, sounded the plop of star-shells sent up by the enemy in futile hope of penetrating the viscid fog. And everywhere was heard the shuffle and stumbling of innumerable boots.

At last the noise of feet began to die away, and the uneven groping tread of the twelve Americans to sound more distinctly for the lessening of the surrounding turmoil. And in another few seconds Bruce came to a halt--not to an abrupt stop, as when he had allowed an enemy squad to pass in front of him, but a leisurely checking of speed, to denote that he could go no farther with the load he was helping to haul.

Mahan put out his free hand. It encountered the American wires. Bruce had stopped at the spot where the party had cut a narrow path through the entanglement on the outward journey. Alone, the dog could easily have passed through the gap, but he could not be certain of pulling Mahan with him. Wherefore the halt.

The last of the twelve men scrambled down to

safety, in the American first-line trench, Bruce among them. The lieutenant went straight to his commanding officer, to make his report. Sergeant Mahan went straight to his company cook, whom he woke from a snoreful sleep. Presently Mahan ran back to where the soldiers were gathered admiringly around Bruce.

The Sergeant carried a chunk of fried beef, for which he had just given the cook his entire remaining stock of cigarettes.

"Here you are, Bruce!" he exclaimed. "The best in the shop is none too good for the dog that got us safe out of that filthy mess. Eat hearty!"

Bruce did not so much as sniff at the (more or less) tempting bit of meat. Coldly he looked up at Mahan. Then, with sensitive ears laid flat against his silken head, in token of strong contempt, he turned his back on the Sergeant and walked away.

Which was Bruce's method of showing what he thought of a human fool who would give him a command and who would then hold so tightly to him that the dog could hardly carry out the order.

CHAPTER V

The Double Cross

In the background lay a landscape that had once been beautiful. In the middle distance rotted a village that had once been alive. In the foreground stood an edifice that had once been a church. The once-beautiful landscape had the look of a gigantic pockmarked face, so scored was it by shell-scar and crater. Its vegetation was swept away. Its trees were shattered stumps. Its farmsteads were charred piles of rubble.

The village was unlike the general landscape, in that it had never been beautiful. In spite of globe-trotters' sentimental gush, not all villages of northern France were beautiful. Many were built for thrift and for comfort and for expediency; not for architectural or natural loveliness.

But this village of Meran-en-Laye was not merely deprived of what beauty it once might or might not have possessed. Except by courtesy it was no longer a village at all. It was a double row of squalid ruins, zig-zagging along the two sides of what was left of its main street. Here and there a cottage or tiny shop or shed was still habitable. The rest was debris.

The church in the foreground was recognizable as such by the shape and size of its ragged walls, and by a half-smashed image of the Virgin and Child which slanted out at a perilous angle above its façade.

Yet, miserable as the ruined hamlet seemed to the casual eye, it was at present a vacation-resort--and a decidedly welcome one--to no less than three thousand tired men. The wrecked church was an impromptu hospital beneath whose shattered roof dozens of these men lay helpless on makeshift cots.

For the mixed American and French regiment known as the "Here-We- Comes" was billeted at Meran-en-Laye during a respite from the rigors and perils of the front-line trenches.

The rest and the freedom from risks, supposed to be a part of the "billeting" system, were not wholly the portion of the "Here-We

Comes." Meran--en--Laye was just then a somewhat important little speck on the warmap.

The Germans had been up to their favorite field sport of trying to split in half two of the Allied armies, and to roll up each, independently. The effort had been a failure; yet it had come so near to success that many railway communications were cut off or deflected. And Meran-en-Laye had for the moment gained new importance, by virtue of a spur railway-line which ran through its outskirts and which made junction with a new set of tracks the American engineers were completing. Along this transverse of roads much ammunition and food and many fighting men were daily rushed.

The safety of the village had thus become of much significance. While it was too far behind the lines to be in grave danger of enemy raids, yet such danger existed to some extent. "Wherefore the presence of the "Here-We-Comes"--for the paradoxical double purpose of "resting up" and of guarding the railway Function.

Still, it was better than trench-work; and the "Here-We-Comes" enjoyed it--for a day or so. Then trouble had set in.

A group of soldiers were lounging on the stone seat in front of the village estaminet. Being off duty, they were reveling in that popular martial pastime known to the Tommy as "grousing" and to the Yankee doughboy as "airing a grouch."

Top-Sergeant Mahan, formerly of the regular army, was haranguing the others. Some listened approvingly, others dissentingly and others not at all.

"I tell you," Mahan declared for the fourth time, "somebody's double-crossing us again. There's a leak. And if they don't find out where it is, a whole lot of good men and a million dollars' worth of supplies are liable to spill out through that same leak. It--"

"But," argued his crony, old Sergeant Vivier, in his hard- learned English, "but it may all be of a chance, mon vieux. It may, not be the doubled cross,--whatever a doubled cross means,-- but the mere chance. Such things often--"

"Chance, my grandmother's wall-eyed cat!" snorted Mahan. "Maybe it might have been chance--when this place hadn't been bombed for a month--for a whole flight of boche artillery and airship grenades to cut loose against it the day General Pershing happened to stop here for an hour on his way to Chateau-Thierry. Maybe that was chance--though I know blamed well it wasn't. Maybe it was chance that the place wasn't bombed again till two days ago, when that troop-train had to spend such a lot of time getting shunted at the junction. Maybe it was chance that the church, over across the street, hadn't been touched since the last drive, till our regiment's wounded were put in it--and that it's been hit three times since then. Maybe any one of those things-- and of a dozen others was chance. But it's a cinch that ALL of them weren't chance. Chance doesn't work that way. I--"

"Perhaps," doubtfully assented old Vivier, "perhaps. But I little like to believe it. For it means a spy. And a spy in one's midst is like to a snake in one's blankets. It is a not pleasing comrade. And it stands in sore need of killing."

"there's spies everywhere," averred Mahan. "That's been proved often enough. So why not here? But I wish to the Lord I could lay hands on him! If this was one of the little sheltered villages, in a valley, his work would be harder. And the boche airships and the long-rangers wouldn't find us such a simple target. But up here on this ridge, all a spy has to do is to flash a signal, any night, that a boche airman can pick up or that can even be seen with good glasses from some high point where it can be relayed to the German lines. The guy who laid out this burg was sure thoughtless. He might have known there'd be a war some day. He might even have strained his mind and guessed that we'd be stuck here. Gee!"

He broke off with a grunt of disgust; nor did he so much as listen to another of the group who sought to lure him into an opinion as to whether the spy might be an inhabitant of the village or a camp-follower.

Sucking at his pipe; the Sergeant glowered moodily down the ruined street. The village drowsed under the hot midday. Here and there a soldier lounged along aimlessly or tried out his exercise-book French on some puzzled, native. Now and then an officer passed in or out of the half-unroofed mairie which served as regimental headquarters.

Beyond, in the handkerchief-sized village square, a platoon was drilling. A thin French housewife was hanging sheets on a line behind a shell-twisted hovel. A Red Cross nurse came out of the hospital--church across the street from the estaminet and seated herself on the stone steps with a basketful of sewing.

Mahan's half-shut eyes rested critically on the drilling platoon--amusedly on the woman who was so carefully hanging the ragged sheets,--and then approvingly upon the Red Cross nurse on the church steps across the way.

Mahan, like most other soldiers, honored and revered the Red Cross for its work of mercy in the army. And the sight of one of the several local nurses of the Order won from him a glance of real approbation.

But presently into his weather-beaten face came an expression of glad welcome. Out of the mairie gate and into the sleepy warmth of the street lounged a huge dark-brown-and-white collie. The don stretched himself lazily, fore and aft, in true collie style, then stood gazing about him as if in search of something of interest to occupy his bored attention.

"Hello!" observed Mahan, breaking in on a homily of Vivier's. "There's Bruce!"

Vivier's leathery face brightened at sound of the collie's name. He looked eagerly in the direction of Mahan's pointing finger.

"Ce brave!" exclaimed the Frenchman. "I did not know even that he was in the village. It must be he is but new-arriven. Otherwise he would, of an assuredly, have hunted up his old friends. Ohe, Bruce!" he called invitingly.

"The big dog must have gotten here just a few minutes ago," said Sergeant Mahan. "He was coming out of headquarters when I saw him. That must mean he's just struck the town, and with a message for the K.O. He always goes like greased lightning when he's on dispatch duty, till he has delivered his message. Then, if he's to be allowed to hang around a while before he's sent back, he loafs, lazy-like; the way you see him now. If all the courier- dogs were like him, every human courier would be out of a job."

At Vivier's hail the great collie had pricked his ears and glanced inquiringly up and down the street. Catching sight of the group seated in front of the estaminet, he began to wag his plumy tail and set off toward them at a trot.

Ten minutes earlier, Bruce had cantered into
Meran-en-Laye from the opposite end of the street,
bearing in his collar a dispatch from the corps
commander to the colonel of the "Here-We-
Comes." The colonel, at the mairie, had read the
dispatch and had patted its bearer; then had bidden
the dog lie down and rest, if he chose, after his long
run.

Instead, Bruce had preferred to stroll out in search
of friends.

Top-Sergeant Mahan, by the way, would have felt
highly flattered had he chanced to get a glimpse of
the dispatch Bruce had brought to the colonel. For it
bore out Mahan's own theory regarding the
presence of spies at or near the village, and it bade
the "Here- We-Come" colonel use every means for
tracing them.

It added the information that three troop-trains with
nine engines were to pass through the village that
night on their way to the trenches, and that the
trains were due at the junction at nine o'clock or
shortly thereafter. The mairie was on the other side
of the street from the estaminet. Incidentally, it was
on the shady side of the street--for which reason
Bruce,--being wise, and the day being hot,--
remained on that side, until he should come
opposite the bench where his friends awaited him.

His course, thus, brought him directly past the
church.

As he trotted by the steps, the Red Cross nurse, who

sat sewing there, chirped timidly at him. Bruce
paused in his leisurely progress to see who had
accosted him whether an old acquaintance, to be
greeted as such, or merely a pleasantly inclined
stranger.

His soft brown eyes rested first in idle inquiry upon
the angular and white-robed figure on the steps.
Then, on the instant, the friendly inquiring look left
his eyes and their softness went with it--leaving the
dog's gaze cold and frankly hostile.

One corner of Bruce's lips slowly lifted, revealing a
tiny view of the terrible white fangs behind them.
His gayly erect head was lowered, and in the depths
of his furry throat a growl was born. When a dog
barks and holds his head up, there is little enough to
fear from him. But when he lowers his head and
growl--then look out.

Mahan knew dogs. In stark amazement he now
noted Bruce's strange attitude toward the nurse.
Never before had he seen the dog show active
hostility toward a stranger--least of all toward a
stranger who had in no way molested him. It was
incredible that the wontedly dignified and sweet-
tempered collie had thus returned a greeting.
Especially from a woman!

Mahan had often seen Red Cross nurses stop to
caress Bruce. He had been amused at the dog's
almost protective cordiality toward all women,
whether the French peasants or the wearers of the
brassard of mercy.

Toward men--except those he had learned to look
on as friends-- the collie always comported himself
with a courteous aloofness But he had seemed to
regard every woman as something to be humored
and guarded and to be treated with the same cordial
friendliness that he bestowed on their children--
which is the way of the best type of collie. Yet
Bruce had actually snarled at this woman who had
chirped to him from the steps of the church! And he
showed every sign of following up the challenge by
still more drastic measures.

"Bruce!" called Mahan sharply. "BRUCE! Shame!
Come over here! Come, NOW!"

At the Sergeant's vehement summons Bruce turned
reluctantly away from the foot of the church steps
and came across the street toward the estaminet. He
came slowly. Midway he halted and looked back
over his shoulder at the nurse, his fangs glinting
once more in a snarl. At a second and more
emphatic call from Mahan the dog continued his
progress.

The nurse had started back in alarm at the collie's
angry demonstration. Now, gathering up her work,
she retreated into the church.

"I'm sorry, Miss!" Mahan shouted after her. "I never
saw him that way, before, when a lady spoke to
him. If it was any dog but old Bruce, I'd give him a
whaling for acting like that to you. I'm dead-sure he
didn't mean any harm."

"Oh, I was going in, anyway," replied the nurse,

from the doorway. "It is of no consequence."

She spoke nervously, her rich contralto voice shaken by the dog's fierce show of enmity. Then she vanished into the church; and Mahan and Vivier took turns in lecturing Bruce on his shameful dearth of courtesy.

The big dog paid no heed at all to his friends' discourse. He was staring sullenly at the doorway through which the nurse had gone.

"That's one swell way for a decently bred dog to treat a woman!" Mahan was telling him. "Least of all, a Red Cross nurse! I'm clean ashamed of you!"

Bruce did not listen. In his heart he was still angry-- and very much perplexed as well. For he knew what these stupid humans did not seem to know.

HE KNEW THE RED CROSS NURSE WAS NO WOMAN AT ALL, BUT A MAN.

Bruce knew, too, that the nurse did not belong to his loved friends of the Red Cross. For his uncanny power of scent told him the garments worn by the impostor belonged to some one else. To mere humans, a small and slender man, who can act, and who dons woman's garb, is a woman. To any dog, such a man is no more like a woman than a horse with a lambskin saddle-pad is a lamb. He is merely a man who is differently dressed from other men-- even as this man who had chirped to Bruce, from the church steps, was no less a man for the costume in which he had swathed his body. Any dog, at a glance and at a sniff, would have known that.

Women, for one thing, do not usually smoke dozens of rank cigars daily for years, until their flesh is permeated with the smell of tobacco. A human could not have detected such a smell--such a MAN-smell,--on the person who had chirped to Bruce. Any dog, twenty feet away, would have noticed it, and would have tabulated the white-clad masquerader as a man. Nor do a woman's hair and skin carry the faint but unmistakable odor of barracks and of tent-life and of martial equipment, as did this man's. The masquerader was evidently not only a man but a soldier.

Dogs,--high-strung dogs,--do not like to have tricks played on them; least of all by strangers. Bruce seemed to take the nurse-disguise as a personal affront to himself. Then, too, the man was not of his own army. On the contrary, the scent proclaimed him one of the horde whom Bruce's friends so manifestly hated--one of the breed that had more than once fired on the dog.

Diet and equipment and other causes give a German soldier a markedly different scent, to dogs' miraculously keen nostrils,-- and to those of certain humans,--from the French or British or American troops. War records prove this. Once having learned the scent, and having learned to detest it, Bruce was not to be deceived.

For all these reasons he had snarled loathingly at the man in white. For these same reasons he could not readily forget the incident, but continued every now and then to glance curiously across toward the church.

Presently,--not relishing the rebukes of the friends who had heretofore pestered him by overmuch petting,--the collie arose quietly from his couch of trampled earth at the foot of the stone bench and strolled back across the street. Most of the men were too busy, talking, to note Bruce's departure. But Sergeant Mahan caught sight of him just as the dog was mounting the last of the steps leading into the church.

As a rule, when Bruce went investigating, he walked carelessly and with his tail slightly a-wag. Now his tail was stiff as an icicle, and he moved warily, on the tips of his toes. His tawny- maned neck was low. Mahan, understanding dogs, did not like the collie's demeanor. Remembering that the nurse had entered the church a few minutes earlier, the Sergeant got to his feet and hastily followed Bruce.

The dog, meanwhile, had passed through the crazily splintered doorway and had paused on the threshold of the improvised hospital, as the reek of iodoform and of carbolic smote upon his sensitive nostrils. In front of him was the stone-paved vestibule. Beyond was the interior of the shattered church, lined now with double rows of cots.

Seated on a camp-chair in the shadowy vestibule was the pseudo Red Cross nurse. At sight of the collie the nurse got up in some haste. Bruce, still walking stiff-legged, drew closer.

Out from under the white skirt flashed a capable
and solidly- shod foot. In a swinging kick, the foot
let drive at the oncoming dog. Before Bruce could
dodge or could so much as guess what was coming,-
-the kick smote him with agonizing force, square on
the shoulder.

To a spirited collie, a kick carries more than the
mere pain of its inflicting. It is a grossly
unforgivable affront as well--as many a tramp and
thief have learned, at high cost.

By the time the kick had fairly landed, Bruce had
recovered from his instant of incredulous surprise;
and with lightning swiftness he hurled himself at his
assailant.

No bark or growl heralded the murderous
throatlunge. It was all the more terrible for the
noiselessness wherewith it was delivered. The
masquerading man saw it coming, just too late to
guard against it. He lurched backward, belatedly
throwing both hands up to defend his throat. It was
the involuntary backward step which saved his
jugular. For his heel caught in the hem of his white
skirt. And wholly off balance, he pitched headlong
to the floor.

This jerky shift of position, on the part of the foe,
spoiled Bruce's aim. His fearful jaws snapped
together harmlessly in empty air at a spot where, a
fraction of a second earlier, the other's throat had
been. Down crashed the disguised man. And atop of
him the furious dog hurled himself, seeking a
second time the throatgrip he had so narrowly

missed.

At this point on the program Sergeant Mahan
arrived just in time to bury both hands in the mass
of Bruce's furry ruff and to drag the snarlingly rabid
dog back from his prey.

The place was in an uproar. Nurses and doctors
came rushing out into the vestibule; sick and
wounded men sat up on their cots and eagerly
craned their necks to catch sight of the scrimmage.
Soldiers ran in from the street.

Strong as he was, Mahan had both hands full in
holding the frantic Bruce back from his enemy.
Under the insult of the kick from this masquerader,
whom he had already recognized as a foe, the collie
had temporarily lost every vestige of his stately
dignity. He was for the moment merely a wild beast,
seeking revenge for a brutal injury. He writhed and
fought in Mahan's grasp. Never once did he seek to
attack the struggling man who held him. But he
strained every giant sinew to get at the foe who had
kicked him.

The dog's opponent scrambled to his feet, helped by
a dozen willing hands and accosted by as many
solicitous voices. The victim's face was bone-gray
with terror. His lips twitched convulsively. Yet, as
befitted a person in his position, he had a splendid
set of nerves. And almost at once he recovered
partial control over himself.

"I--I don't know how it happened," he faltered, his
rich contralto voice shaky with the ground-swells of

his recent shock. "It began when I was sitting on the steps, sewing. This dog came past. He growled at me so threateningly that I came indoors. A minute later, while I was sitting here sewing, he sprang at me and threw me down. I believe he would--would have killed me," the narrator finished, with a very genuine shudder, "if I had not been rescued when I was. Such bloodthirsty brutes ought to be shot!"

"He not only OUGHT to be," hotly agreed the chief surgeon, "but he is GOING to be. Take him out into the street, one of you men, and put a ball in his head."

The surgeon turned to the panting nurse.

"You're certain he didn't hurt you?" he asked. "I don't want a newcomer, like yourself, to think this is the usual treatment our nurses get. Lie down and rest. You look scared to death. And don't be nervous about the cur attacking you again. He'll be dead inside of three minutes."

The nurse, with a mumbled word of thanks, scuttled off into the rear of the church, where the tumbledown vestry had been fitted up as a dormitory.

Bruce had calmed down somewhat under Mahan's sharp reproof. But he now struggled afresh to get at his vanished quarry. And again the Sergeant had a tussle to hold him.

"I don't know what's got into the big fellow!" exclaimed Mahan to Vivier as the old Frenchman joined the tumultuous group. "He's gone clean daft. He'd of killed that poor woman, if I hadn't--"

"Get him out of here!" ordered the surgeon. "And clear out, yourselves, all of you! This rumpus has probably set a lot of my patients' temperatures to rocketing. Take the cur out and shoot him!"

"Excuse me, sir," spoke up Mahan, as Vivier stared aghast at the man who commanded Bruce's destruction, "but he's no cur. He's a courier-collie, officially in the service of the United States Government. And he's the best courier-dog in France to-day. This is--"

"I don't care what he is!" raged the surgeon. "He--"

"This is Bruce," continued Mahan, "the dog that saved the 'Here- We-Comes' at Rache, and that steered a detail of us to safety one night in the fog, in the Chateau-Thierry sector. If you order any man of the 'Here-We-Comes' to shoot Bruce, you're liable to have a mutiny on your hands--officer or no officer. But if you wish, sir, I can transmit your order to the K.O. If he endorses it--"

But the surgeon sought, at that moment, to save the remnants of his dignity and of a bad situation by stalking loftily back into the hospital, and leaving Mahan in the middle of his speech.

"Or, sir," the Sergeant grinningly called after him, "you might write to the General Commanding, and tell him you want Bruce shot. The Big Dog always sleeps in the general's own room, when he's off-

duty, at Division Headquarters. Maybe the general
will O.K. his death-sentence, if you ask him to. He--
"

Somewhat quickening his stately stride, the surgeon
passed out of earshot. At the officers' mess of the
"Here-We-Comes," he had often heard Bruce's
praises sung. He had never chanced to see the dog
until now. But, beneath his armor of dignity, he
quaked to think what the results to himself must
have been, had he obeyed his first impulse of
drawing his pistol and shooting the adored and
pricelessly useful collie.

Mahan,--stolidly rejoicing in his victory over the
top-lofty potentate whom he disliked,--led the way
out of the crowded vestibule into the street. Bruce
followed demurely at his heels and Vivier
bombarded everybody in sight for information as to
what the whole fracas was about.

Bruce was himself again. Now that the detested
man in woman's clothes had gone away, there was
no sense in continuing to struggle or to waste
energy in a show of fury. Nevertheless, in his big
heart burned deathless hatred toward the German
who had kicked him. And, like an elephant, a collie
never forgets.

"But," Vivier was demanding of everybody, "but
why should the gentle Bruce have attacked a good
nurse? It is not what you call 'make-sense.' C'est un
gentilhomme, ce vieux! He would not attack a
woman less still a sister of the Red Cross. He--"

"Of course he wouldn't," glumly assented the downhearted Mahan. "But he DID. That's the answer. I saw him do it. He knocked her down and-_"

"Which nurse was she?" asked a soldier who had come up after the trouble was over.

"A new one here. I don't know her name. She came last week. I saw her when she got here. I was on duty at the K.O.'s office when she reported. She had a letter from some one on the surgeon- general's staff. But why Bruce should have gone for her to-day-- or for any woman--is more than I can see. She was scared half to death. It's lucky she heard the surgeon order him shot. She'll suppose he's dead, by now. And that'll cure her scare. We must try to keep Bruce away from this end of the street till he goes back to headquarters to-morrow."

As a result Bruce was coaxed to Mahan's company-shed and by dint of food-gifts and petting was induced to spend most of the day there.

At sunset Bruce tired of his dull surroundings. Mahan had gone on duty; so had Vivier; so had others of his friends. The dog was bored and lonely. Also he had eaten much. And a walk is good, not only for loneliness, but for settling an overfull stomach. Bruce decided to go for a walk.

Through the irregular street of the village he picked his way, and on toward the open country beyond. A sentry or two snapped fingers of greeting to him as he strolled past them. The folk of the village eyed his bulk and graceful dignity with something like awe.

Beyond the hamlet the ridge of hilltop ran on for perhaps a quarter-mile before dipping into the plain below. At one end of this little plateau a company of infantry was drilling. Bruce recognized Mahan among the marching lines, but he saw his friend was on duty and refrained from going up to him.

Above, the sunset sky was cloudless. Like tiny specks, miles to eastward, a few enemy airships circled above the heap of clustered hills which marked the nearest German position. The torn-up plain, between, seemed barren of life. So, at first, did the farther end of the jutting ridge on which the village was perched. But presently Bruce's idly wandering eye was caught by a flutter of white among some boulders that clumped together on the ridge's brow farthest from the village.

Some one--a woman, from the dress--was apparently picking her way through the boulders. As Bruce moved forward, a big rock shut her off from his view and from the view of the hamlet and of the maneuvering infantry company a furlong away.

Just then a puff of breeze blew from eastward toward the collie; and it bore to him a faint scent that set his ruff a-bristle and his soft brown eyes ablaze. To a dog, a scent once smelled is as recognizable again as is the sight of a once-seen face to a human. Bruce set off at a hand-gallop toward the clump of boulders.

The Red Cross nurse, whom Bruce had so nearly killed, was off duty until the night-shift should go on at the hospital. The nurse had taken advantage of this brief surcease from toil, by going for a little walk in the cool sunset air, and had carried along a bag of sewing.

Up to three months ago this nurse had been known as Heinrich Stolz, and had been a valued member of the Wilhelmstrasse's workingforce of secret agents. Then, acting under orders, Herr Heinrich Stolz had vanished from his accustomed haunts. Soon thereafter a Red Cross nurse--Felicia Stuart by name had reported for duty at Paris, having been transferred thither from Italy, and bearing indubitable credentials to that effect.

From carefully picked-up information Stolz had just learned of the expected arrival of the three troop-trains at the junction at nine that evening. The tidings had interested him keenly, and he knew of other people to whom they would be far more interesting.

Seating himself under the lee of the easternmost rock, Stolz primly opened his sewing-bag and drew forth various torn garments. The garments were for the most part white, but one or two were of gaudy colors.

By way of precaution, in case of discovery, the spy threaded a needle. Thus, if any one should chance to see him shake out a garment, preparatory to laying it on his knee and mending it, there could be no reasonable cause for suspicion. Herr Stolz was nothing if not efficient.

He held up the needle and poked the thread at its eye in truly feminine fashion.

He had just finished this feat of dexterity when he chanced to look up from his work at sound of fast-pattering feet. Not thirty feet away, charging head on at him, rushed the great brown-and- white collie he supposed had been shot.

With a jump of abject terror, Herr Stolz sprang up. Mingled with his normal fear of the dog was a tinge of superstitious dread. He had been so certain the beast was shot! The doctor had given the order for his killing. The doctor was a commissioned officer. Stolz's German mind could not grasp the possibility of a soldier disobeying an officer's imperative command.

The collie was upon him by the time the spy gained his feet. Stolz reached frantically under his dress-folds for the deadly little pistol that he always kept there. But he was still a novice in the mysteries of feminine apparel. And, before his fingers could close on the weapon, Bruce's bared fangs were gleaming at his throat.

Stolz ceased to search for the weapon. And, as before, he threw up both frantic hands to ward off the furious jaws.

He was barely in time. Bruce's white teeth drove deep into the spy's forearm, and Bruce's eighty pounds of furry muscular bulk smote Stolz full in the chest. Down went the spy, under the terrific impact, sprawling wildly on his back, and fighting with both bleeding hands to push back the dog.

Bruce, collie-fashion, did not stick to one grip, but bit and slashed a dozen times in three seconds, tearing and rending his way toward the throat-hold he craved; driving through flesh of hands and of forearms toward his goal.

Like many another German, Stolz was far more adept at causing pain than at enduring it. Also, from birth, he had had an unconquerable fear of dogs. His nerves, too, were not yet recovered from Bruce's attack earlier in the day. All this, and the spectral suddenness of the onslaught, robbed him of every atom of his usual stony self-control.

Sergeant Mahan was a good soldier. Yet a minute earlier he had almost ruined his reputation as such. He had been hard put to it to refrain from leaving the ranks of his drilling company, a furlong from the rocks, and running at record speed toward the boulders. For he had seen the supposed nurse pass that way. And almost directly afterward he had seen Bruce follow her thither. And he could guess what would happen.

Luckily for the sake of discipline, the order of "Break ranks!" was given before Mahan could disgrace himself by such unmartial behavior. And, on the instant, the Sergeant broke into a run in the direction of the rocks.

Wondering at his eccentric action, several of the

soldiers followed. The company captain, at sight of
a knot of his men dashing at breakneck speed
toward the boulders, started at a more leisurely pace
in the same direction.

Mahan had reached the edge of the rocks when his
ears were greeted by a yell of mortal fear. The
captain and the rest, catching the sound, went faster.
Screech after screech rang from the rocky
enclosure.

Mahan rounded the big boulder at the crest of the
ridge and flung himself upon the two combatants, as
they thrashed about in a tumultuous dual mass on
the ground. And just then Bruce at last found his
grip on Stolz's throat.

A stoical German signal-corps officer, on a hilltop
some miles to eastward, laid aside his field--glass
and calmly remarked to a man at his side

"We have lost a good spy!"

Such was the sole epitaph and eulogy of Herr
Heinrich Stolz, from his army.

Meantime, Sergeant Mahan was prying loose the
collie's ferocious jaws from their prey and was
tugging with all his might to drag the dog off the
shrieking spy. The throat-hold, he noted, was a bare
inch from the jugular.

The rest of the soldiers, rushing up pell-mell, helped
him pull the infuriated Bruce from his victim. The
spectacle of their admired dog-hero, so murderously

mauling a woman of the Red Cross, dazed them with horror.

"Take him AWAY!" bellowed Stolz, delirious with pain and fear. "He's KILLED me--der gottverdammte Teufelhund!"

And now the crazed victim's unconscious use of German was not needed to tell every one within hearing just who and what he was. For the quavering tones were no longer a rich contralto. They were a throaty baritone. And the accent was Teutonic.

"Bruce!" observed Top-Sergeant Mahan next morning, "I've always said a man who kicks a dog is more of a cur than the dog is. But you'll never know how near I came to kicking you yesterday, when I caught you mangling that filthy spy. And Brucie, if I had kicked you, well--I'd be praying at this minute that the good Lord would grow a third leg on me, so that I could kick myself all the way from here to Berlin!"

CHAPTER VI.

The Werewolf

When Bruce left the quiet peace of The Place for the hell of the Western Front, it had been stipulated by the Mistress and the Master that if ever he were disabled, he should be shipped back to The Place, at their expense.

It was a stipulation made rather to soothe the
Mistress's sorrow at parting from her loved pet than
in any hope that it could be fulfilled; for the average
life of a courierdog on the battle- front was
tragically short. And his fate was more than
ordinarily certain. If the boche bullets and shrapnel
happened to miss him, there were countless
diseases--bred of trench and of hardship and of
abominable food--to kill him.

The Red Cross appeal raised countless millions of
dollars and brought rescue to innumerable human
warriors. But in caring for humans, the generosity
of most givers reached its limit; and the Blue Cross-
-"for the relief of dogs and horses injured in the
service of the Allies"--was forced to take what it
could get. Yet many a man, and many a body of
men, owed life and safety to the heroism of some
war-dog, a dog which surely merited special care
when its own certain hour of agony struck.

Bruce's warmest overseas friends were to be found
in the ranks of the mixed Franco-American
regiment, nicknamed the "Here-We-Comes." Right
gallantly, in more than one tight place, had Bruce
been of use to the "Here-We-Comes." On his
official visits to the regiment, he was always
received with a joyous welcome that would have
turned any head less steady than a thoroughbred
collie's.

Bruce enjoyed this treatment. He enjoyed, too, the
food-dainties wherewith the "Here-We-Comes"
plied him. But to no man in the army would he give
the adoring personal loyalty he had left at The Place

with the Mistress and the Master. Those two were still his only gods. And he missed them and his sweet life at The Place most bitterly. Yet he was too good a soldier to mope.

For months the "Here-We-Comes" had been quartered in a "quiet"--or only occasionally tumultuous--sector, near Chateau-Thierry. Then the comparative quiet all at once turned to pandemonium.

A lanky and degenerate youth (who before the war had been unlovingly known throughout Europe as the "White Rabbit" and who now was mentioned in dispatches as the "Crown Prince") had succeeded in leading some half-million fellow-Germans into a "pocket" that had lately been merely a salient.

From the three lower sides of the pocket, the Allies ecstatically flung themselves upon their trapped foes in a laudable effort to crush the half-million boches and their rabbit-faced princeling into surrender before the latter could get out of the snare, and to the shelter of the high ground and the reenforcements that lay behind it. The Germans objected most strenuously to this crushing process. And the three beleaguered edges of the pocket became a triple-section of hell.

It was a period when no one's nerves were in any degree normal-- least of all the nerves of the eternally hammered Germans. Even the fiercely advancing Franco-Americans, the "Here-We-Comes," had lost the grimly humorous composure that had been theirs, and waxed sullen and ferocious in their eagerness.

Thus it was that Bruce missed his wontedly
uproarious welcome as he cantered, at sunset one
July day, into a smashed farmstead where his
friends, the "Here-We-Comes," were bivouacked
for the night. By instinct, the big dog seemed to
know where to find the temporary regimental
headquarters.

He trotted past a sentry, into an unroofed cattle-
shed where the colonel was busily scribbling a
detailed report of the work done by the "Here-We-
Comes" during that day's drive.

Coming to a halt by the colonel's side, Bruce stood
expectantly wagging his plumy tail and waiting for
the folded message from division headquarters to be
taken off his collar.

Usually, on such visits, the colonel made much of
the dog. To-day he merely glanced up abstractedly
from his writing, at sight of Bruce's silken head at
his side. He unfastened the message, read it,
frowned and went on with his report.

Bruce continued to wag his tail and to look up
wistfully for the wonted petting and word of
commendation. But the colonel had forgotten his
existence. So presently the collie wearied of waiting
for a caress from a man whose caresses, at best, he
did not greatly value. He turned and strolled out of
the shed. His message delivered, he knew he was at
liberty to amuse himself as he might choose to, until
such time as he must carry back to his general a

reply to the dispatch he had brought.

From outside came the voices of tired and lounging soldiers. A traveling kitchen had just been set up near by. From it arose a blend of smells that were mighty tempting to a healthily hungry dog. Thither, at a decorous but expectant pace, Bruce bent his steps.

Top-Sergeant Mahan was gazing with solicitous interest upon the toil of the cooks at the wheeled kitchen. Beside him, sharing his concern in the supper preparations, was Mahan's closest crony, old Sergeant Vivier. The wizened little Frenchman, as a boy, had been in the surrender of Sedan. Nightly, ever since, he had besought the saints to give him, some day, a tiny share in the avenging of that black disgrace.

Mahan and Vivier were the warmest of Bruce's many admirers in the "Here-We-Comes." Ordinarily a dual whoop of joy from them would have greeted his advent. This afternoon they merely chirped abstractedly at him, and Mahan patted him carelessly on the head before returning to the inspection of the cooking food.

Since an hour before dawn, both men had been in hot action. The command for the "Here-We-Comes" to turn aside and bivouac for the night had been a sharp disappointment to them, as well as to every unwounded man in the regiment.

When a gambler is in the middle of a winning streak, when an athlete feels he has the race in his

own hands, when a business man has all but closed
the deal that means fortune to him--at such crises it
is maddening to be halted at the very verge of
triumph. But to soldiers who, after months of
reverses, at last have their hated foe on the run, such
a check does odd things to temper and to nerves.

In such plight were the men of the "Here-We-
Comes," on this late afternoon. Mahan and Vivier
were too seasoned and too sane to give way to the
bursts of temper and the swirls of blasphemy that
swayed so many of their comrades. Nevertheless
they were glum and silent and had no heart for jolly
welcomings,--even to so dear a friend as Bruce.

Experience told them that a square meal would
work miracles in the way of calming and bracing
them. Hence, apart from stark hunger, their interest
in the cooking of supper.

Bruce was too much a philosopher--and not devoted
enough to his soldier friends--to be hurt at the lack
of warmth in the greeting. With the air of an
epicure, he sniffed at the contents of one of the
kitchen's bubbling kettles. Then he walked off and
curled himself comfortably on a pile of bedding,
there to rest until supper should be ready.

Several times, as he lay there, soldiers passed and
repassed. One or two of them snapped their fingers
at the dog or even stooped, in passing, to stroke his
head. But on the faces of all of them was unrest and
a certain wolfish eagerness, which precluded
playing with pets at such a time. The hot zest of the
man-hunt was upon them. It was gnawing in the

veins of the newest recruit,

ever, as in the heart of the usually self-contained colonel of the regiment.

The colonel, in fact, had been so carried away by the joy of seeing his men drive the hated graycoats before them that day that he had overstepped the spirit of his own orders from the division commander.

In brief, he had made no effort to "dress" his command, in the advance, upon the regiments to either side of it. As a result, when the signal to bivouac for the night was given, the "Here-We-Comes" were something like a mile ahead of the regiment which should have been at their immediate right, and nearly two miles in front of the brigade at their left.

In other words, the "Here-We-Comes" now occupied a salient of their own, ahead of the rest of the FrancoAmerican line. It was in rebuke for this bit of good progress and bad tactics that the division commander had written to the colonel, in the dispatch which Bruce had brought.

German airmen, sailing far above, and dodging as best they could the charges of the Allied 'planes, had just noted that the "Here- We-Comes" "salient" was really no salient at all. So far had it advanced that, for the moment, it was out of touch with the rest of the division. It was, indeed, in an excellent position to be cut off and demolished by a dashing nightattack. And a report to this effect was delivered to a fumingly distracted German major general, who yearned for a chance to atone in some way for the day's shameful reverses.

"If they hadn't halted us and made us call it a day, just as we were getting into our stride," loudly grumbled one Yankee private to another as the two clumped up to the kitchen, "we'd have been in Fere-en-Tardenois by now. What lazy guy is running this drive, anyhow?"

"The same lazy guy that will stick you into the hoosgow for insubordination and leave you to do your bit there while the rest of us stroll on to Berlin!" snapped Top-Sergeant Mahan, wheeling upon the grumbler. "Till you learn how to obey orders without grouching, it isn't up to you to knock wiser men. Shut up!"

Though Mahan's tone of reproof was professionally harsh, his spirit was not in his words. And the silenced private knew it. He knew, too, that the top-sergeant was as savage over the early halt as were the rest of the men.

Bruce, as a rule, when he honored the "Here-We-Comes" with a visit, spent the bulk of his time with Mahan and old Vivier. But to-day neither of these friends was an inspiring companion. Nor were the rest of Bruce's acquaintances disposed to friendliness. Wherefore, as soon as supper was eaten, the dog returned to his heap of bedding, for the hour or so of laziness which Nature teaches all her children to demand, after a full meal,--and which the so-called "dumb" animals alone are intelligent enough to take.

Dusk had merged into night when Bruce got to his feet again. Taps had just sounded. The tired men gladly rolled themselves into their blankets and fell into a dead sleep. A sentry-relief set forth to replace the first batch of sentinels with the second.

Mahan was of the party. Though the topsergeant had been a stupid comrade, thus far to-day, he was now evidently going for a walk. And even though it was a duty-walk, yet the idea of it appealed to the dog after his long inaction.

So Bruce got up and followed. As he came alongside the stiffly marching top-sergeant, the collie so far subverted discipline as to thrust his nose, in friendly greeting, into Mahan's slightly cupped palm. And the top-sergeant so far abetted the breach of discipline as to give the collie's head a furtive pat. The night was dim, as the moon had not risen; so the mutual contact of good-fellowship was not visible to the marching men on either side of Mahan and the dog. And discipline, therefore, did not suffer much, after all.

At one post after another, a sentinel was relieved and a fresh man took his place. Farthest in front of the "Here-We-Comes" lines-- and nearest to the German--was posted a lanky Missourian whom Bruce liked, a man who had a way of discovering in his deep pockets stray bits of food which he had hoarded there for the collie and delighted to dole out to him. The Missourian had a drawlingly soft voice the dog liked, and he used to talk to Bruce as if the latter were another human.

For all these reasons--and because Mahan was too busy and too grumpy to bother with him--Bruce elected to stay where he was, for a while, and share the Missourian's vigil. So, when the rest of the party moved along to the next sentry-go, the dog remained. The Missourian was only too glad to have him do so. It is tedious and stupid to pace a desolate beat, alone, at dead of night, after a day of hard fighting. And the man welcomed the companionship of the dog.

For a time, as the Missourian paced his solitary stretch of broken and shrub-grown ground, Bruce gravely paced to and fro at his side. But presently this aimless promenade began to wax uninteresting. And, as the two came to the far end of the beat, Bruce yawned and lay down. It was pleasanter to lie there and to watch the sentinel do the walking.

Stretched out, in a little grass-hollow, the dog followed blinkingly with his soft brown eyes the pendulumlike progress of his friend. And always the dog's plumed tail would beat rhythmic welcome against the ground as the sentry approached him.

Thus nearly an hour wore on. A fat moon butted its lazy way through the smoke-mists of the eastern skyline.

Then something happened--something that Bruce could readily have forestalled if the wind had been blowing from the other direction, and if a dog's eyes were not as nearsighted as his nose is farsmelling.

The Missourian paused to run his hand caressingly over the collie's rough mane, and moved on, down the lonely beat. Bruce watched his receding figure, drowsily. At the end of ninety yards or more, the Missourian passed by a bunch of low bushes which grew at the near side of a stretch of hilly and shellpocked ground. He moved past the bushes, still watched by the somewhat bored dog.

It was then that Bruce saw a patch of bushshadow detach itself from the rest, under the glow of the rising moon. The shadow was humpy and squat. Noiseless, it glided out from among the bushes, close at the sentry's heels, and crept after him.

Bruce pricked his ears and started to get up. His curiosity was roused. The direction of the wind prevented him from smelling out the nature of the mystery. It also kept his keen hearing from supplying any clue. And the distance would not permit him to see with any distinctness.

Still his curiosity was very mild. Surely, if danger threatened, the sentinel would realize it. For by this time the Shadow was a bare three feet behind him near enough, by Bruce's system of logic, for the Missourian to have smelled and heard the pursuer. So Bruce got up, in the most leisurely fashion, preparatory to strolling across to investigate. But at almost his first step he saw something that changed his gracefully slouching walk into a charging run.

The Shadow suddenly had merged with the sentinel. For an instant, in stark silence, the two seemed to cling together. Then the Shadow fled, and the lanky

Missourian slumped to the earth in a sprawling
heap, his throat cut.

The slayer had been a deft hand at the job. No
sound had escaped the Missourian, from the
moment the stranglingly tight left arm had been
thrown around his throat from behind until, a
second later, he fell bleeding and lifeless.

In twenty leaping strides, Bruce came up to the
slain sentinel and bent over him. Dog-instinct told
the collie his friend had been done to death. And the
dog's power of scent told him it was a German who
had done the killing.

For many months, Bruce had been familiar with the
scent of German soldiers, so different from that of
the army in which he toiled. And he had learned to
hate it, even as a dog hates the vague "crushed
cucumber" smell of a pitviper. But while every dog
dreads the viper-smell as much as he loathes it,
Bruce had no fear at all of the boche odor. Instead,
it always awoke in him a blood-lust, as fierce as any
that had burned in his wolf- ancestors.

This same fury swept him now, as he stood,
quivering, above the body of the kindly man who so
lately had petted him; this and a craving to revenge
the murder of his human friend.

For the briefest time, Bruce stood there, his dark
eyes abrim with unhappiness and bewilderment, as
he gazed down on the huddled form in the wet
grass. Then an electric change came over him. The
softness fled from his eyes, leaving them bloodshot

and blazing. His great tawny ruff bristled like an angry cat's. The lazy gracefulness departed from his mighty body. It became tense and terrible. In the growing moonlight his teeth gleamed whitely from under his upcurled lip.

In a flash he turned and set off at a loping run, nose close to ground, his long stride deceptively swift. The zest of the man- hunt had obsessed him, as completely as, that day, it had spurred the advance of the "Here-We-Comes."

The trail of the slayer was fresh, even over such broken ground. Fast as the German had fled, Bruce was flying faster. Despite the murderer's long start, the dog speedily cut down the distance between his quarry and himself. Not trusting to sight, but solely to his unerring sense of smell. Bruce sped on.

Then, in a moment or two, his hearing re-enforced his scent. He could catch the pad-pad-pad of running feet. And the increasing of the sound told him he was gaining fast.

But in another bound his ears told him something else--something he would have heard much sooner, had not the night wind been setting so strongly in the other direction. He heard not only the pounding of his prey's heavy-shod feet, but the soft thud of hundreds--perhaps thousands--of other army shoes. And now, despite the adverse wind, the odor of innumerable soldiers came to his fiercely sniffing nostrils. Not only was it the scent of soldiers, but of German soldiers.

For the first time, Bruce lifted his head from the ground, as he ran, and peered in front of him. The moon had risen above the low-lying horizon vapors into a clear sky, and the reach of country was sharply visible.

Bruce saw the man he was chasing,--saw him plainly. The German was still running, but not at all as one who flees from peril. He ran, rather, as might the bearer of glad tidings. And he was even now drawing up to a group of men who awaited eagerly his coming. There must have been fifty men in the group. Behind them--in open formation and as far as the dog's near-sighted eyes could see-- were more men, and more, and more--thousands of them, all moving stealthily forward.

Now, a collie (in brain, though never in heart) is much more wolf than dog. A bullterrier, or an Airedale, would have charged on at his foe, and would have let himself be hacked to pieces before loosing his hold on the man.

But--even as a wolf checks his pursuit of a galloping sheep when the latter dashes into the guarded fold--Bruce came to an abrupt halt, at sight of these reenforcements. He stood irresolute, still mad with vengeful anger, but not foolish enough to assail a whole brigade of armed men.

It is quite impossible (though Mahan and Vivier used to swear it must be true) that Bruce had the reasoning powers to figure out the whole situation which confronted him. He could not have known that a German brigade had been sent to take advantage of the "Here-We-Comes" temporarily isolated position--that three sentries had been killed in silence and that their deaths had left a wide gap through which the brigade hoped to creep unobserved until they should be within striking distance of their unsuspectingly slumbering victims.

Bruce could not have known this. He could not have grasped the slightest fraction of the idea, being only a real-life dog and not a fairytale animal. But what he could and did realize was that a mass of detested Germans was moving toward him, and that he could not hope to attack them, single-handed; also, that he was not minded to slink peacefully away and leave his friend unavenged.

Thwarted rage dragged from his furry throat a deep growl; a growl that resounded eerily through that silent place of stealthy moves. And he stepped majestically forth from the surrounding long grass, into the full glare of moonlight.

The deceptive glow made him loom gigantic and black, and tinged his snowy chest with the phosphorous gleam of a snowfield. His eyes shone like a wild beast's.

Corporal Rudolph Freund, of the Konigin Luise Regiment, had just finished his three-word report to his superior. He had merely saluted and announced

"He is dead!"

Corporal Freund did not thrill, as usual, to the colonel's grunt of approval. The Corporal was

worried. He was a Black Forest peasant; and, while
iron military life had dulled his native superstitions,
it had not dispelled them.

The night was mystic, in its odd blend of moon and
shadows. However hardened one may be, it is a
nerve-strain to creep through long grass, like a red
Indian, to the murder of a hostile sentinel. And
every German in the "Pocket" had been under
frightful mental and physical stress, for the past
week.

Corporal Rudolph Freund was a brave man and a
brute. But that week had sapped his nerve. And the
work of this night had been the climax. The
desolate ground, over which he had crawled to the
killing, had suddenly seemed peopled with evil
gnomes and goblins, whose existence no true Black
Forest peasant can doubt. And, on the run back, he
had been certain he heard some unseen monster
tearing through the underbrush in hot pursuit of
him. So certain had he been, that he had redoubled
his speed.

There were no wolves or other large wild animals in
that region. When he had wriggled toward the slow-
pacing American sentinel, he had seen and heard no
creature of any sort. Yet he was sure that on the way
back he had been pursued by--by Something! And
into his scared memory, as he ran, had flashed the
ofttold Black Forest tale of the Werewolf--the
devil--beast that is entered by the soul of a
murdered man and which tracks the murderer to his
death.

Glad was the unnerved Corporal Freund when his run ceased and he stood close to his grossly solid and rank-scented fellowmen once more. Almost he was inclined to laugh at his fears of the fabled Werewolf--and especially at the idea that he had been pursued. He drew a long breath of relief. He drew the breath in. But he did not at once expel it. For on his ears came the sound of a hideous menacing growl.

Corporal Freund spun about, in the direction of the mysterious threat. And there, not thirty feet from him, in the ghostly moonlight, stood the Werewolf!

This time there could be no question of overstrained nerves and of imagination. The Thing was THERE!

Horribly visible in every detail, the Werewolf was glaring at him. He could see the red glow of the gigantic devil-beast's eyes, the white flash of its teeth, the ghostly shimmering of its snowy chest. The soul of the man he had slain had taken this traditional form and was hunting down the slayer! A thousand stories of Freund's childhood verified the frightful truth. And overwrought human nature's endurance went to pieces under the shock.

A maniac howl of terror split the midnight stillness. Shriek after shriek rent the air. Freund tumbled convulsively to the ground at his colonel's feet, gripping the officer's booted knees and screeching for protection. The colonel, raging that the surprise attack should be imperiled by such a racket, beat the frantic man over the mouth with his heavy fist, kicking ferociously at his upturned writhing face, and snarling to him to be silent.

The shower of blows brought Freund back to sanity, to the extent of changing his craven terror into Fear's secondary phase--the impulse to strike back at the thing that had caused the fright. Rolling over and over on the ground, under the impact of his superior's fist blows and kicks, Freund somehow regained his feet.

Reeling up to the nearest soldier, the panic-crazed corporal snatched the private's rifle and fired three times, blindly, at Bruce. Then, foaming at the mouth, Freund fell heavily to earth again, chattering and twitching in a fit.

Bruce, at the second shot, leaped high in the air, and collapsed, in an inert furry heap, among the bushes. There he lay,--his career as a courier-dog forever ended.

Corporal Rudolph Freund was perhaps the best sniper in his regiment. Wildly though he had fired, marksman-instinct had guided his bullets. And at such close range there was no missing. Bruce went to earth with one rifle ball through his body, and another in his leg. A third had reached his skull.

Now, the complete element of surprise was all-needful for the attack the Germans had planned against the "Here-We-Comes." Deprived of that advantage the expedition was doomed to utter failure. For, given a chance to wake and to rally, the regiment could not possibly be "rushed," in vivid moonlight, before the nearest Allied forces could move up to its support. And those forces were only a mile or so to the rear. There can be no possible hope for a surprise attack upon a well-appointed camp when the night's stillness has been shattered by a series of maniac screams and by three echoing rifle-shots.

Already the guard was out. A bugle was blowing. In another minute, the sentry-calls would locate the gap made by the three murdered sentinels.

A swift guttural conference among the leaders of the gray-clad marauders was followed by the barking of equally guttural commands. And the Germans withdrew as quietly and as rapidly as they had come.

It was the mouthing and jabbering of the fit-possessed Corporal Rudolph Freund that drew to him the notice of a squad of Yankees led by Top-Sergeant Mahan, ten minutes later. It was the shudder --accompanied pointing of the delirious man's finger, toward the nearby clump of undergrowth, that revealed to them the still warm body of Bruce.

Back to camp, carried lovingly in Mahan's strong arms, went all that was left of the great courier-dog. Back to camp, propelled between two none-too-gentle soldiers, staggered the fit-ridden Corporal Freund.

At the colonel's quarters, a compelling dose of stimulant cleared some of the mists from the prisoner's brain. His nerve and his will-power still gone to smash, he babbled eagerly enough of the night attack, of the killing of the sentries and of his encounter with the Werewolf.

"I saw him fall!" he raved. "But he is not dead. The Werewolf can be killed only by a silver bullet, marked with a cross and blessed by a priest. He will live to track me down! Lock me where he cannot find me, for the sake of sweet mercy!"

And in this way, the "Here-We-Comes" learned of Bruce's part in the night's averted disaster.

Old Vivier wept unashamed over the body of the dog he had loved. Top-Sergeant Mahan--the big tears splashing, unnoted, from his own red eyes-- besought the Frenchman to strive for better self- control and not to set a cry-baby example to the men.

Then a group of grim-faced soldiers dug a grave. And, carried by Mahan and Vivier, the beautiful dog's body was borne to its resting-place. A throng of men in the gray dawn stood wordless around the grave. Some one shamefacedly took off his hat. With equal shamefacedness, everybody else followed the example.

Mahan laid the dog's body on the ground, at the grave's brink. Then, looking about him, he cleared his throat noisily and spoke.

"Boys," he began, "when a human dies for other humans, there's a Christian burial service read over him. I'd have asked the chaplain to read one over

Bruce, here, if I hadn't known he'd say no. But the Big Dog isn't going to rest without a word said over his grave, for all that."

Mahan cleared his throat noisily once more, winked fast, then went on:--

"You can laugh at me, if any of you feel like it. But there's some of you here who wouldn't be alive to laugh, if Bruce hadn't done what he did last night. He was only just a dog--with no soul, and with no life after this one, I s'pose. So he went ahead and did his work and took the risks, and asked no pay.

"And by and by he died, still doing his work and asking no pay.

"He didn't work with the idea of getting a cross or a ribbon or a promotion or a pension or his name in the paper or to make the crowd cheer him when he got back home, or to brag to the homefolks about how he was a hero. He just went ahead and WAS a hero. That's because he was only a dog, with no soul--and not a man.

"All of us humans are working for some reward, even if it's only for our pay or for the fun of doing our share. But Bruce was a hero because he was just a dog, and because he didn't know enough to be anything else but a hero.

"I've heard about him, before he joined up with us. I guess most of us have. He lived up in Jersey, somewhere. With folks that had bred him. I'll bet a year's pay he was made a lot of by those folks; and

that it wrenched 'em to let him go. You could see
he'd been brought up that way. Life must 'a' been
pretty happy for the old chap, back there. Then he
was picked up and slung into the middle of this hell.

"So was the rest of us, says you. But you're wrong.
Those of us that waited for the draft had our choice
of going to the hoosgow, as 'conscientious
objectors,' if we didn't want to fight. And every
mother's son of us knew we was fighting for the
Right; and that we was making the world a decenter
and safer place for our grandchildren and our
womenfolks to live in. We didn't brag about God
being on our side, like the boches do. It was enough
for us to know WE was on GOD'S side and fighting
His great fight for Him. We had patriotism and
religion and Right, behind us, to give us strength.

"Brucie hadn't a one of those things. He didn't know
what he was here for--and why he'd been pitched
out of his nice home, into all this. He didn't have a
chance to say Yes or No. He didn't have any
spellbinders to tell him he was making the world
safe for d'mocracy. He was MADE to come.

"How would any of us humans have acted, if a deal
like that had been handed to us? We'd 'a' grouched
and slacked and maybe deserted. That's because
we're lords of creation and have souls and brains
and such. What did Bruce do? He jumped into this
game, with bells on. He risked his life a hundred
times; and he was just as ready to risk it again the
next day.

"Yes, and he knew he was risking it, too. There's

blame little he didn't know. He saw war-dogs, all
around him, choking to death from gas, or
screaming their lives out, in No Man's Land, when a
bit of shell had disemboweled 'em or a bullet had
cracked their backbones. He saw 'em starve to
death. He saw 'em one bloody mass of scars and
sores. He saw 'em die of pneumonia and mange and
every rotten trench disease. And he knew it might
be his turn, any time at all, to die as they were
dying; and he knew the humans was too busy
nursing other humans, to have time to spare on
caring for tortured dogs. (Though those same dogs
were dying for the humans, if it comes to that.)

"Yes, Bruce knew what the end was bound to be.
He knew it. And he kept on, as gay and as brave as
if he was on a day's romp. He never flinched. Not
even that time the K.O. sent him up the hill for
reenforcements at Rache, when every sharpshooter
in the boche trenches was laying for him, and when
the machine guns were trained on him, too. Bruce
knew he was running into death--,then and a dozen
other times. And he went at it like a white man.

"I'm--I'm getting longwinded. And I'll stop. But--
maybe if you boys will remember the Big Dog--and
what he did for us,--when you get back home,--if
you'll remember him and what he did and what
thousands of other war-dogs have done,--then
maybe you'll be men enough to punch the jaw of
any guy who gets to saying that dogs are nuisances
and that vivisection's a good thing, and all that. If
you'll just do that much, then--well, then Bruce
hasn't lived and died for nothing!

"Brucie, old boy," bending to lift the tawny body and lower it into the grave, "it's good-by. It's good-by to the cleanest, whitest pal that a poor dub of a doughboy ever had. I--"

Mahan glowered across at the clump of silent men.

"If anybody thinks I'm crying," he continued thickly, "he's a liar. I got a cold, and--"

"Sacre bon Dieu!" yelled old Vivier, insanely. "Regarde-donc! Nom d'une pipe!"

He knelt quickly beside the body, in an ecstasy of excitement. The others craned their necks to see. Then from a hundred throats went up a gasp of amazement.

Bruce, slowly and dazedly, was lifting his magnificent head!

"Chase off for the surgeon!" bellowed Mahan, plumping down on his knees beside Vivier and examining the wound in the dog's scalp. "The bullet only creased his skull! It didn't go through! It's just put him out for a few hours, like I've seen it do to men. Get the surgeon! If that bullet in his body didn't hit something vital, we'll pull him around, yet! GLORY BE!"

It was late summer again at The Place, late opulent summer, with the peace of green earth and blue sky, the heavy droning of bees and the promise of harvest. The long shadows of late afternoon stretched lovingly across the lawn, from the great lakeside trees. Over everything brooded a dreamy amber light. The war seemed a million miles away.

The Mistress and the Master came down from the vine-shaded veranda for their sunset walk through the grounds. At sound of their steps on the gravel, a huge dark-brown-and-white collie emerged from his resting-place under the wistaria-arbor.

He stretched himself lazily, fore and aft, in collie-fashion. Then he trotted up to his two deities and thrust his muzzle playfully into the Mistress's palm, as he fell into step with the promenaders.

He walked with a stiffness in one foreleg. His gait was not a limp. But the leg's strength could no longer be relied on for a ten-mile gallop. Along his forehead was a new-healed bullet- crease. And the fur on his sides had scarcely yet grown over the mark of the high-powered ball which had gone clear through him without touching a mortal spot.

Truly, the regimental surgeon of the "Here-We-Comes" had done a job worthy of his own high fame! And the dog's wonderful condition had done the rest.

Apart from scars and stiffness, Bruce was none the worse for his year on the battle-front. He could serve no longer as a dashing courier. But his life as a pet was in no way impaired.

"Here's something that came by the afternoon mail, Bruce," the Master greeted him, as the collie ranged alongside. "It belongs to you. Take a look at it."

The Master drew from his pocket a leather box, and opened it. On the oblong of white satin, within the cover, was pinned a very small and very thin gold medal. But, light as it was, it had represented much abstinence from estaminets and tobacco-shops, on the part of its donors.

"Listen," the Master said, holding the medal in front of the collie. "Listen, while I read you the inscription: 'To Bruce. From some of the boys he saved from the boches.'"

Bruce was sniffing the thin gold lozenge interestedly. The inscription meant nothing to him. But--strong and vivid to his trained nostrils--he scented on the medal the loving finger- touch of his old friend and admirer, Top Sergeant Mahan.

Made in the USA
Middletown, DE
19 December 2019